S0-AGF-666

Massachusetts
State Facts

Nickname:	Bay State
Date Entered Union:	February 6, 1788 (the 6th state)
Motto:	*Ense petit placidam sub libertate quietem* (By the sword we seek peace, but peace only under liberty)
Massachusetts Men:	John Fitzgerald Kennedy, *U.S. president* Cecil B. DeMille, *film director* Benjamin Franklin, *statesman and scientist* Winslow Homer, *painter* Theodor Geisel (Dr. Seuss), *author and illustrator*
Flower:	Mayflower
Bird:	Chickadee
Fun Fact:	*The official state dessert of Massachusetts is Boston cream pie *The Fig Newton™ was named after Newton, Massachusetts

"All I can say is, fires are a hell of a lot more predictable than women."

—Zach Chapin

* * * *

"I'm not some wimpy dame who's going to be a drag on you, Zach. I can hold my own. You have my word that you won't have to be picking me up off the floor...."

—Rebecca Fox

American HEROES
AGAINST ALL ODDS

ELISE TITLE
Body Heat

HARLEQUIN®

TORONTO • NEW YORK • LONDON
AMSTERDAM • PARIS • SYDNEY • HAMBURG
STOCKHOLM • ATHENS • TOKYO • MILAN • MADRID
PRAGUE • WARSAW • BUDAPEST • AUCKLAND

If you purchased this book without a cover you should be aware
that this book is stolen property. It was reported as "unsold and
destroyed" to the publisher, and neither the author nor the
publisher has received any payment for this "stripped book."

HARLEQUIN BOOKS
225 Duncan Mill Road, Don Mills,
Ontario, Canada M3B 3K9

ISBN 0-373-82219-7

BODY HEAT

Copyright © 1994 by Elise Title

All rights reserved. Except for use in any review, the reproduction or
utilization of this work in whole or in part in any form by any electronic,
mechanical or other means, now known or hereafter invented, including
xerography, photocopying and recording, or in any information storage
or retrieval system, is forbidden without the written permission of the
publisher, Harlequin Enterprises Limited, 225 Duncan Mill Road,
Don Mills, Ontario, Canada M3B 3K9.

All characters in this book have no existence outside the imagination of
the author and have no relation whatsoever to anyone bearing the same
name or names. They are not even distantly inspired by any individual
known or unknown to the author, and all incidents are pure invention.

This edition published by arrangement with Harlequin Books S.A.

® and TM are trademarks of the publisher. Trademarks indicated with
® are registered in the United States Patent and Trademark Office, the
Canadian Trade Marks Office and in other countries.

Visit us at www.eHarlequin.com

Printed in U.S.A.

About the Author

Elise Title grew up in New York City and received her M.S.W. in clinical social work from the University of California at Berkeley. She is the author of fifty-five romance novels—thirty of them for Harlequin and Silhouette—and has received numerous awards. In1991-92 she was awarded the *Romantic Times Magazine* Certificate of Excellence for Innovative Series Romance. She was chosen as one of the Favorite Top Ten Authors by readers of *Affaire de Coeur.* In 1991-92 her book *Making It* was awarded the *Romantic Times Magazine* Reviewer's Choice Award for Best Harlequin Temptation, and she won this award again in 1994-95 for *Dangerous at Heart.*

Elise currently lives in Massachusetts, where *Body Heat* is set, and is working on a couple of screenplays—with her twenty-six-year-old son—and more novels!

Books by Elise Title

Harlequin Temptation

Love Letters #203
Baby, It's You! #223
MacNamara and Hall #266
Too Many Husbands #282
Making It #340
Jack and Jill #358
Adam & Eve #412
For the Love of Pete #416
True Love #420
Taylor Made #424
Just the Way You Are #438
You Were Meant for Me #455
Body Heat #473
Dangerous at Heart #509
Heartstruck #513
Heart to Heart #517

Harlequin American Romance

Till the End of Time #377
Nearly Paradise #397

Harlequin Superromance

Out of the Blue #363
Trouble in Eden #478
Meg & the Mystery Man #618

Harlequin Intrigue

Circle of Deception #97
All Through the Night #119
The Face in the Mirror #149
Shadow of the Moon #160
Stage Whispers #180
No Right Turn #209

Mira

Hot Property

Silhouette Shadows
Who is Deborah? #2

Dear Reader,

Before becoming a writer, I was a prison psychotherapist in Massachusetts. I treated murderers, burglars, rapists and, yes, arsonists. There was always the potential for danger.

When I started writing romance novels, I did a 180-degree turn. Instead of dealing with "bad guys," I created love stories with a good dose of humor, sex and adventure. Guess you could say I was "burned out." I loved writing sexy romantic comedies. But danger is in my blood. Ultimately, I couldn't resist also writing stories that sizzled with both passion and mayhem. *Body Heat* has heavy doses of both, showing how the good guy—and the "good gal"—get the bad guy, and how the good guy also gets the good gal.

And Zach Chapin is your all-time "good guy." Okay, I fall a little bit in love with all my romance heroes, but I confess Zach tops my list. He's not only your tall, dark and handsome romantic hero, he's a true hero who risks his life to save others; who faces danger head-on; who's daring, compelling, undaunted, and he's got a wry sense of humor, to boot. Plus, he knows how to make love with a capital *L.* Just ask Rebecca Fox, a woman who's a perfect "match" for Zach. Together, they could set the world on fire. And nearly do!

Fondly,

Elise Title

_____ Prologue _____

FADE IN

EXTERIOR: DOORWAY—PITTSBURGH—NIGHT

A dark figure in a black coat, collar pulled up and fedora pulled down, lurks in the shadows. Only his breath is visible in the cold night air. Headlights illuminate the figure for a moment, and we get a brief flash of his eyes—intense, excited, a little crazy.

CAMERA PULLS BACK and we see fancy cars and limos pulling up to a swank town house across the street. Men and women dressed in elegant evening wear are assisted out of their cars by young valets, and then proceed to enter the town house which is all lit up for a party.

INTERIOR: TOWN HOUSE—NIGHT

A formal cocktail party is in full swing. A jazz combo is playing in the main sitting room. A few couples are dancing, others mingle in clusters in that room and in the grand foyer. Waiters and waitresses circulate, offering champagne and canapés to the guests.

CUT TO FOYER

ALICE WITHERSPOON, the fiftyish hostess is greeting new arrivals. An aristocratic-looking couple in their early forties approaches. They are Alderman VINCENT GRAUMAN and his wife, SUZANNE. Alice busses them each on both cheeks.

ALICE

Vincent, Suzanne, how wonderful that you could make it.

VINCE

We wouldn't miss one of your bashes for the world, Alice.

SUZANNE

The place looks terrific, Alice. Who was your decorator?

ALICE
(coyly)
I imported him from Rome.

They move off as Alice rushes to greet another new guest, MAYOR MARTIN STELLMAN, a dapper man in his early sixties.

ALICE

Mayor Stellman, what a pleasure to see you.

MAYOR

I'm up to my neck in committee meetings, but I promised you I'd make an appearance, and I always keep my word.

ALICE

That's why you'll always get my vote.

She slips an arm through his, smiling flirtatiously at him.

ALICE

And my full support.

MAYOR

I count on that, Alice. Can we have a few words in private before I put politics aside for the evening?

They head for the closed doors that lead to the library. As the doors open, there is a strange hiss and then a heavy, thunderous roar as flames explode before Alice and the mayor. Flames billowing over them, the erupting wall of fire literally lifts them off their feet and flings them backward into the foyer.

Nearby, a few guests witness what's happening and start screaming. Those in the parlor initially don't react—not seeing or hearing anything over the din of the music and conversation. When they do, there is utter chaos. As the fire begins to spread, people start shrieking and racing for windows, doors. Flames engulf the whole house....

EXTERIOR: DOORWAY—NIGHT

Sounds of laughter emanate from the doorway where a figure in black is standing. Then he steps out into the street and races down the street away from the fire. We can still faintly hear his laughter until it's drowned out by approaching sirens.

EXTERIOR: FIRE STATION—DAY

Weary, exhausted, soot-covered fire fighters are putting equipment away. TONI PARADISI, a striking-looking brunette in her mid-twenties enters. She's dressed in a plain business suit—the skirt short enough to showcase her very shapely legs. The fire fighters don't look happy to see her as she stops to have a few words with a couple of them. They shrug and shake their heads. She doesn't seem bothered by their lack of response. As she heads off for an office marked Bureau of Fire Investigation, two of the fire fighters snicker.

> FIRE FIGHTER 1
>
> Wanna bet she don't last too long on the arson squad now that Stellman's out of the picture?

> FIRE FIGHTER 2
>
> Wanna bet the rest of the squad won't be cryin' in their beer?

> FIRE FIGHTER 1
>
> Of course, she could hit it off with Stellman's replacement and end up commissioner.

Toni's about to walk into the office when she turns around and smiles at the two fire fighters who hadn't realized they'd been overheard.

> TONI
>
> That could happen, boys. You never know.

INTERIOR: BUREAU OF FIRE INVESTIGATIONS—DAY

Six fire marshals are sitting at assorted shabby desks when Toni enters the dreary, green-walled, fluorescent-lit room. She perches herself on the edge of her partner's desk. JOHN NOONAN, a beefy-looking Irishman in his mid-fifties, looks up from a fire report he's writing.

> TONI
>
> You ready to go check out the Witherspoon place?

He doesn't respond. The other fire marshals get real busy with paperwork.

> TONI
>
> Okay, Noonan, just level with me.

Noonan motions with his thumb to a corner cubicle, marked William Bowers, Chief Fire Marshal.

> NOONAN
> Bowers is handling this one himself…with his own handpicked team.

> TONI
> His own handpicked team, huh…

> NOONAN
> Don't go flying off the handle, Toni. Everyone's on edge about this one, what with the mayor and a half-dozen very influential folk going up in smoke.

> TONI
> I never fly off the handle.

She storms off for the cubicle. One of the fire marshals snickers to the guy next to him.

> FIRE MARSHAL 1
> Nah, she don't fly *off* the handle. She flies *on* it.

> TONI
> (not looking back)
> I heard that crack.

INTERIOR: BOWERS'S CUBICLE—DAY

WILLIAM BOWERS, a ruggedly handsome man in his mid-thirties gives Toni a steely look.

> BOWERS
> This one's real ugly, Paradisi.

TONI
Since when couldn't I handle ugly, Bowers?

BOWERS
We got half a dozen crispers lying in that mess.
One of them is our very own mayor. Believe me,
Toni, you don't want to be in on this one.

TONI
I'm not mourning Stellman any more than anybody else in this building and you know it, Billy.
You think I don't know he's been trying to sandbag us, shut us down, and hand all arson investigations over to the police department? There's no
love lost between me and Stellman. Never was.

Bowers rises and approaches Toni. They stare at each
other in silence. Then suddenly, he pulls her into his
arms and kisses her. She responds eagerly, taking hold
of his hand and guiding it down over her buttocks.

TONI
Does this mean you're handpicking me, Chief?

BOWERS
That's been my problem from the start, baby. I
can't seem to keep my hands off you.
He lifts her up onto his desk as he kisses her again,
a framed photo getting knocked over. The camera
zeroes in on the photo—a family picture of Bowers, his pert blond wife, and two kids....

1

REBECCA FOX WAS SPRAWLED out on a mint-green cushioned chaise on the poolside patio of her Malibu beach house. After a couple of minutes she set the script she was reading down across her thighs, lifted her sunglasses, and gave the squat, middle-aged, balding man who had been both her agent and her good friend for over five years a wary look. "I hope it's not going to be all sex and no action."

"Call me old-fashioned, but I always thought the two were synonymous," Sam Porter teased. He was sitting across from her on a matching chaise, an unlit cigar wedged between his lips. He knew better than to light up around his favorite client who was always on his case to quit smoking, not to mention give up saturated fats, get more exercise, and, to Sam's way of thinking, basically give up everything that was any fun.

Rebecca, wearing a wisp of a white bikini, rubbed some more sunscreen on her golden skin. "Seriously, Sam, the last supposed action screenplay you made me plow through, the heroine spent one-third of her time seducing the hero into bed, one-third of her time in bed with him, and one-third of the time pleading with him not to get out of bed to go off and nab the bad guys. Which, of course, he did anyway. No doubt, Bill Lake will get nominated for an Academy Award for his efforts. And what do you suppose Kelly Moore will get for hers? Probably one of the many nighties she'll get to wear on the set. Tell me, do you think she'll place her 'award' on her mantelpiece?"

Sam grinned. "Okay, so *Danger Zone* wasn't exactly your cup of tea. It was still a good part. Moore grabbed it up in a flash. Nighties and all."

"Fine," Rebecca said firmly. "She can have it. I want a part with some substance. Some relevance. Mostly, I want a part where I'm not the dutiful wife, the decorative girlfriend, the other woman, or the whore with a heart of gold. I want to be more than window dressing, Sam."

She glanced back down at the script. "Why does Bowers have to be married?"

"Rebecca..."

"Okay, but kids? I'll have half the women in the audience hating me for being a home wrecker."

Sam smiled at her. The smile was only half-paternal. Okay, so he'd been happily married for twenty-four years and Rebecca was young enough to be his daughter. But, hell, he was only human. "Honey, you'll have every man in the audience..."

Rebecca held up her hand to stop him from completing the sentence.

Sam clammed up, but the twinkle in his eye didn't fade. He knew how hard Rebecca was struggling against her image as a movie sex goddess, but when you were nearly six feet tall with brown bedroom eyes the size of saucers, a cascade of wavy auburn hair, a bone structure that would have had the famous sculptor, Rodin, drooling, and every luscious curve of her body in precisely the right place, it wasn't easy to concentrate on her acting ability. Not that the twenty-six-year-old star couldn't act rings around most actresses. It was just that she rarely got the kinds of parts that highlighted her talent.

"Read the rest of the script," he coaxed. "It's hot, Rebecca. The part of Toni is exactly what you've been looking for. She doesn't take a back seat to anyone, Bowers included. She's the one who gets to track the arsonist down, risking life and limb to do it. Toni is tough, savvy, daring. Brains as well as beauty. Brave yet vulnerable. On top of that, the character is very centered."

Rebecca grinned. "You know just the right buttons to push, Sam."

"Read, read."

As Rebecca returned to the script, out of the corner of her eye she noticed her manager, Gail McCarthy, pop out onto the patio. Gail, a slender, plain-looking twenty-eight-year-old, had come to Hollywood seven years ago straight from an all-girls college near her hometown of Scituate, south of Boston. She'd started out as a secretary at a talent-management firm, but her skill in dealing with "difficult" personalities soon became apparent and she was quickly promoted. Rebecca had hired Gail to be her personal manager three years ago. Though the two of them were as different as day and night, they got along famously.

Gail glanced at the script. "'Blue Fire'?"

Rebecca gave a distracted nod. She was reading faster and faster, her excitement mounting. "This is good," she muttered, flipping to the next page. Halfway down the page, she tapped her finger. "Now, this is what I'm talking about. The scene where Paradisi goes into the morgue to view the mayor. Gutsy stuff."

Gail smiled slyly at Sam as she dropped some papers on a glass-topped table before heading back inside. "She likes it. By Jove, she likes it."

Sam winked.

After skimming through the rest of the script, Rebecca slapped it down on her lap, her eyes sparkling with excitement. "Damn it, Sam, this script is fantastic. Toni Paradisi is the role of a lifetime. She's everything you said. This part could finally prove to everyone in this town that I'm an *actress*. You know what I'm saying, Sam?"

"I know what you're saying, princess."

"So, when do I sign on the dotted line?"

Sam cleared his throat. "Well..."

Rebecca sprang up from the chaise. She grabbed hold of a rose-colored silk kimono hanging on the arm of the chaise and slipped it over her bikini. "Come on, Sam. Mason gave you this script because he wants me, right?"

A red flush rose above the collar of Sam's Gucci shirt. He sat up straight in his chaise. "He's definitely... intrigued."

"Intrigued? Intrigued? What does that mean? And don't go spouting a dictionary definition, Sam. Give it to me straight."

"Sit down."

She stayed put, tapping her foot impatiently. "Sam."

Sam swung his legs down to the ground and sat forward a little. "Look, Rebecca, when this script came across my desk, I knew this was just what you've been searching for. So I had a little talk with Mason. I told him I thought you'd be perfect for Toni."

"And what did he say?"

"Actually...he had...Jill Muir in mind."

"Jill Muir? For Toni? How come he didn't just go with Julia Roberts?"

Sam smiled sheepishly. "She wasn't available."

"What you're really saying is, he doesn't see me in a serious part? I just knew that after I won that dumb Sexiest Actress of the Year award it would be the death knell for me."

Her agent threw up his hands. "What are you talking about? You're a top box-office draw. Writers and directors are coming out of the woodwork with scripts for you."

Rebecca made a face. "I know. I've seen the scripts. The point is, why'd you even have me read this damn one, Sam?"

"Because you've been telling me for over a year now that you want to stretch. And this part is your chance to do just that."

"But…"

"Mason hasn't signed Muir yet. And like I said, he was…intrigued when I told him you were the right actress for the part."

"'Intrigued.' We seem to be going around in circles here, Sam. Cut to the chase."

Sam rubbed his jaw. "You'd have to…audition."

Rebecca blinked at him in disbelief. "Audition? He wants *me* to audition?"

Sam wasn't about to tell her he had to talk Mason into even letting her try out. She would have had a fit. Worse still, he knew that she would have felt absolutely devastated. "I know," he soothed. "You haven't had to audition for a part in three years or more. The thing is, Rebecca, this is a very different kind of role than you've ever played before. I have no doubts, believe me."

"Obviously Mason has doubts." Her voice took on an angry edge. "Why don't you just say it, Sam? He thinks I'm an airhead bimbo who looks great in a negligee, but—"

"Now don't go flying off the handle, Rebecca."

Instead of exploding, which was what Sam fully expected, Rebecca abruptly changed her whole demeanor. She leaned closer to him and smiled sardonically. "I never fly off the handle, Noonan."

Noonan? For a moment, Sam thought Rebecca had come unhinged. Then he remembered that Noonan was a character in "Blue Fire." And Rebecca's remark was a line straight out of the script.

Rebecca's mind shifted into high gear. "How much time do I have?"

"Mason's still looping *Bad Intentions*. He won't be auditioning for three weeks."

Rebecca began to pace. "Three weeks. That doesn't give me much time."

"Time for what?" Sam asked nervously.

"Research, Sam. I've got to get into Toni's skin. I've got to know what it's like to…" Rebecca paused, snatching up the script from the chaise and riffling through the pages until she found what she was looking for. "'Face the animal, taste the soot it leaves behind, live with the heat and the smoke twenty-four hours a day.'"

Gail was standing at the open door. "Say, that's good."

Rebecca sighed. "Not good enough. I need to actually experience what it's like to walk into the burned-out shell of a building, heavy with smoke stains, hunting out where the fire started, what set it off. I need to understand how someone on an arson squad thinks, how he feels, what makes him tick. I need to know what it's like to track down a real, live arsonist. When I show up for that audition in three weeks, I want to *be* Toni Paradisi, arson investigator extraordinaire."

"Well…" Gail began.

Rebecca's gaze shot to her manager. "What? You know someone on an arson squad?"

"Not exactly. I've got a cousin who's a—"

"Fireman? A fireman is good. A fireman's a start."

"A secretary."

"A secretary? Come on, Gail."

Gail smiled smugly at the actress. "She's a secretary to the fire commissioner. In Boston."

"Boston, Rebecca?" Sam intoned.

"What's wrong with Boston?" Rebecca retorted. "I love Boston."

"You've never been to Boston," her agent shot back.

"Okay, but I do love Boston-baked beans," Rebecca said with a grin.

"It would mean you'd be gone over Christmas. And

New Year's Eve. What about the Marcus bash at Spago? You don't want to miss that."

"I won't have to miss it. I'll fly back on the thirtieth. As for Christmas—I'll get to see real snow. It'll be great," she said, hustling Gail over to a phone. "What are we waiting for? Call your cousin."

Gail looked over at Sam.

"Aren't you getting a little carried away, Rebecca?" Sam said.

"I want this part, Sam." She plucked up the receiver and handed it to Gail. "Dial."

ZACH CHAPIN DUG HIS hands into the pockets of his leather bombardier jacket as he braced against the cold Boston Harbor winds. He walked with a slight limp, not usually noticeable except when it was cold and the muscles in his left leg stiffened up. When he got to the burned-out warehouse, steam and smoke were still oozing from the charred remains. He stopped in front of a gray wall covered with graffiti, cupped his hands and lit a cigarette.

Joe Kelly, a short, paunchy, barrel-chested man in his early fifties, got out of his beat-up Oldsmobile Cutlass sedan, carrying a large metal toolbox. As he ambled across the street, he gave his partner a breezy wave with his free hand. Zach smiled back crookedly, his cigarette relegated to the corner of his mouth so he could stuff his hands back in his pockets.

"It's cold as hell out," he muttered, the cigarette bobbing as he spoke.

Joe Kelly chuckled. "You shoulda been here a few hours ago. I bet this spot was plenty hot."

"I'll take a nice white sandy beach in the Caribbean, thanks."

Joe gave his partner a friendly slap on the back. "Not thinking of calling it quits again, are ya?"

Zach's eyes narrowed. "Not until I nail this creep

who's having such a jolly time burning down the city and making us laughingstocks."

"Whoa. Aren't you jumping the gun? We don't know..."

"*I* know," Zach said grimly.

"Another call?"

Zach nodded. "Phoned me at home this time. Twenty minutes ago."

"Let me guess. He didn't stay on the line long enough for you to put through a trace."

"Just told me to inspect some more of his handiwork, had a little chuckle and hung up."

"What gets me is we can't even get at the method to his madness," Joe said derisively. "The guy's got to be cracked. What I don't get is why he always contacts you. Although you did make headlines for our department a few months back when the mayor's office tried to sandbag us."

"Don't think that business's over yet," Zach said soberly. "The P.D. is still in there plugging at the mayor's office. They'd like nothing better than to have all fire-related homicides handed over to them. Which makes nabbing this damn 'torch' all the more crucial."

"He's not making it easy for us, that's for sure."

"Easy or hard, I'm going to get the bastard."

Joe knew that if anyone was going to nail the arsonist, his money was on his partner. Zach Chapin was the best guy on the squad. He might be cynical and disillusioned, but he was as dedicated and determined as they came. Besides, there was no one on the team better at finding the origins and tracing the spread of fires.

Zach scanned the blackened remains of what had once been a toy-company warehouse. "The bastard would burn the place down right before Christmas."

"No holiday spirit," Joe said dryly. "Speaking of which, you and Eileen still planning to spend Christmas with me, Millie and the kids?" He caught a look on

Zach's face, one he was familiar with. "Don't tell me you blew it with Eileen?" Zach's track record with girl-friends wasn't exactly winning.

"No, I didn't blow it," Zach said defensively.

"Millie's making your favorite. Roast goose."

Zach grinned. "Roast, huh?"

"Sorry. Bad choice of words under the circum-stances, I guess."

"Tell Millie I'll be there. Eileen's thinking of spend-ing Christmas with her folks in Milwaukee."

Joe gave Zach a closer scrutiny. "She's cutting out for the holidays?"

"No big deal," Zach retorted. "It's not like we're en-gaged or anything." Which was just the way he liked it. The heartache and loss of one failed marriage was enough for him.

"Don't jump down my throat. I'm just saying that where there's smoke there's usually fire," Joe teased good-naturedly. "Eileen's a nice gal. Even Millie likes her."

Zach took one last drag of his cigarette, then ground it out under the heel of his shoe as he started for the burned-out warehouse. "All I can say is, fires are a hell of a lot more predictable than women."

THE OFFICE WAS LARGE, mahogany paneled and smelled of pipe tobacco. On the walls were rows of framed pho-tographs featuring solemn men in braided, striped and gold-starred uniforms, officials in custom-tailored suits, groupings of yellow-slickered fire fighters in front of shiny red fire trucks. Two large windows faced onto the street. It was a gray, rainy day. Ice clung to the branches of the trees lining Tremont. For a moment, Re-becca thought longingly of the golden Malibu sunshine she'd left behind, but then she focused her full attention on the gentleman sitting across from her.

"This is really so kind of you," she said in that sultry

voice that had won her so many devoted fans. As luck would have it, one of those devoted fans had turned out to be Peter Fitzgerald, Boston's robust sixty-two-year-old fire commissioner.

The commissioner rose and walked around his desk, perching himself on one corner. "Please, I'm flattered that you've chosen us, Miss Fox. You're my favorite actress."

She accepted his compliment with a provocative smile. "Call me Rebecca."

The fire commissioner beamed. "Rebecca. Now, exactly what is it I can do for you, Rebecca?"

She wasted no time getting down to business. "You can tell me who's the best arson investigator you've got in this town."

"That's easy. Zach Chapin," Fitzgerald said emphatically. "Could have been the bureau chief if he'd learned a little diplomacy along the way. Not that I can really see Zach ever going for a desk job. The guy lives, eats, and breathes fire."

Rebecca leaned forward in her seat, crossing one leg over the other. "Tell me more about Zach Chapin, Commissioner."

"What do you want to know about him?" Fitzgerald asked, his eyes glued to her long, shapely legs.

"Everything."

The fire commissioner smiled at her. "Well, now... Chapin's been with the Bureau of Fire Investigations for close to seven years. Before that he was a fireman. One of the best. I first met him when he was fresh out of the academy."

"That's great. Then you should know him quite well," Rebecca said enthusiastically.

Fitzgerald shrugged. "No. I wouldn't say that. I don't know as how anyone really knows Chapin all that well. He's not an easy man to know. I mean, he's the kind of a guy who keeps things close to his chest. Not exactly outgoing, if you know what I mean."

"You make him sound very enigmatic. Surely Chapin's close to someone."

"Maybe his partner, Joe Kelly. I'd say Kelly's probably gotten closer to him than most. Still…"

"What *can* you tell me about Chapin? How about vital statistics? Age, hair color, height…marital status? Things like that."

"That should be easy enough." The commissioner crossed over to a wooden file cabinet and pulled out a file on Zachary Chapin. Returning to his swivel chair, he flipped it open on his desk and began scanning it. "Let's see. Age, thirty-seven; height, six foot one; hair, brown; eyes, hazel." He looked up at Rebecca. "Good-looking devil."

Rebecca leaned forward. "Married?" She was hoping Chapin was unattached. A wife might have a little difficulty with her hubby being partnered with a Hollywood "sex goddess" for a few weeks.

"Divorced three years ago." Fitzgerald looked up, reflectively. "I believe her name was Shirley. No, Cheryl. That was it. Nice gal. Kind of quiet. Met her once or twice at the firemen's ball."

"Kids?"

Fitzgerald checked the file. "No kids. If my memory doesn't fail me, Zach and Cheryl split just before the Drake fire."

"The Drake fire?"

"The Drake was a hotel in the South End. High-class joint once upon a time. Neighborhood changed, place got run-down, rooms started going by the hour instead of the night, if you catch my drift."

Rebecca smiled. "I catch it. Was it the work of an arsonist?"

The fire commissioner nodded. "Chapin got to the scene while the fire was still raging. He spotted this young gal trapped in the building. Decided to play hero and went in himself to rescue her."

"What happened?"

"The stairway collapsed on their way down. He got her out, but…"

"But?"

"She didn't make it. Turned out she wasn't more than fifteen. Some poor runaway gone astray."

"Oh, that's tragic," Rebecca said softly. She rose and walked over to the window. She pressed her palm against the chilled pane of glass.

"It always goes down hard when you lose someone. When it's a kid…well…" Fitzgerald's voice trailed off for a moment before he continued. "Chapin took it especially hard. He blamed himself even though there was nothing he or anyone else could have done. He talked about quitting. Hell, he still talks about it."

She glanced over at the commissioner. "He still can't accept that her death wasn't his fault?"

"I think he hates to admit he's fallible. When it comes down to it, Chapin's probably more infallible than most," Fitzgerald said with a faint smile. "Like I said, he's the best we've got. Probably one of the best in the country."

Rebecca was only half listening. "First he loses his wife, then the girl he's trying to rescue," she reflected as she stared down at the busy street without really seeing it. "It must have been very painful for him." A man with heart, she thought. With sensitivity. Yet tough, brave, feisty. A perfect character upon which to model Toni Paradisi.

"Oh, it was painful, all right," the fire chief was saying. "Not just emotionally. Zach didn't come out of the Drake unscathed. He ended up in the hospital for a few weeks with second-degree burns over a third of his body and a broken leg."

Rebecca turned back to the commissioner. "Did he ever catch the arsonist?"

Fitzgerald smiled. "What do you think?"

ZACH CHAPIN WAS SITTING in the fire commissioner's office and was far from overjoyed to be there. His disbelieving eyes darted from his immediate superior, Chief Fire Marshal Mike Collins, seated beside him, to Fire Commissioner Peter Fitzgerald, who was giving him an officious look from behind his oversize mahogany desk.

"You're kidding," Zach said. Problem was, he knew they weren't the kidding types.

"It's just for a couple of weeks, Chapin," Fitzgerald soothed.

"A couple of weeks? I can't spare a couple of hours. I'm hot on a case—pardon the pun."

Mike Collins, a trim, handsome, clean-cut forty-three-year-old man with toothpaste-commercial white teeth, nodded surreptitiously to the commissioner, then put his hand on the arson investigator's shoulder. "Maybe a couple of weeks off it wouldn't be such a bad idea, Zach. This creep has been playing mind games with you. It's becoming a little too...personal. Besides, if he knows you're off the case, maybe he'll start getting sloppy...."

Zach was furious. "Off the case? No way. And as for this getting personal..."

Collins couldn't quite meet Zach's eyes. "I've already put Adams on it. He'll team with Kelly while you and Miss Fox—"

"Forget it," Zach said adamantly. "Adams is not waltzing in on my case. Let him team up with your little starlet."

"She asked for you personally, Chapin," Fitzgerald said. "Singled you out from all the rest."

Zach got up from his seat. "Some lamebrain movie

star decides she wants to play arson investigator and I'm supposed to feel honored that I'm the lucky sap who gets saddled with her?"

Fitzgerald gave him a dark look. "Rebecca Fox is not some lamebrain movie star, Chapin. She's a bright, articulate actress who takes her work as seriously as you and I take ours."

"Oh, give me a break. Why can't she just read a book?"

"Zach…" Mike Collins started, but the commissioner waved him to silence.

"This isn't a request, Chapin," Fitzgerald said pointedly. "For the next three weeks—"

"You said two weeks."

"Two, three. What's the difference?"

"Seven days," Zach said dryly.

Collins grimaced. His boy wasn't scoring any points with the fire commissioner. Then again, Zach never had been one for the social graces.

"As I was saying, Chapin," Fitzgerald said firmly, "for the next three weeks you'll show Miss Fox the ropes. Nothing too dangerous, mind you. Just the technical stuff, maybe go over some of your old cases, have her sit in on meetings, take her out to a couple of buildings that you've already gone over and know are safe. We don't want anything to happen to Rebecca."

Zach arched an eyebrow. "Rebecca?"

The fire commissioner shot him a cold look. Mike Collins slunk down lower in his seat.

"Which reminds me," Fitzgerald said somberly. "She wants to be incognito while she's here. No one else on the squad is to know she's an actress. She'll come in under the name Rebecca McBride. Wants to be treated like one of the guys."

Zach laughed harshly. Mike Collins hustled him out of the office before they both ended up getting the ax.

2

REBECCA RECOGNIZED HIM as soon as he stepped out of the bureau's inner sanctum into the small, drab reception room where a young woman with bleached blond hair piled high on her head was busily typing up a report. Rebecca stood up from one of the uncomfortable green plastic chairs that adorned the waiting room. Since he didn't look as if he was going to make the first move, Rebecca forged ahead, plastering on one of her winning smiles. "Hi, you must be Zach Chapin. I'm Rebecca...McBride." She leaned a little closer, giving him a conspiratorial look. "Fresh from the...academy." She extended her hand in greeting.

Zach Chapin knew he was in for it, the moment he set eyes on her. Some women were too beautiful for their own good. Even though she'd clearly done her best to downplay her looks for this "gig," Zach put Rebecca Fox at the head of the class.

"The Academy Awards?" Zach asked wryly, giving her hand a look, but not responding to the gesture. He was being deliberately rude, determined to make her see that she'd chosen the wrong guy.

Refusing to be fazed by his bad manners, Rebecca dropped her arm and quickly glanced over at the typist who was still going at the keys. She lowered her voice. "I thought the commissioner explained that I didn't want anyone else to know who I really am. If your associates knew I was a celebrity, they'd make a big fuss and no one would treat me like one of the guys. I really want to blend in." She leaned a little closer. "Do I carry a gun?"

Zach gave her a dark look.

Rebecca shrugged. "Just asking."

He was staring intently at her hair, which she'd pulled back unflatteringly from her face and twisted into a businesslike French knot. "Is that a wig?"

The corners of Rebecca's mouth twitched with irritation. This was going to be harder than she'd anticipated. "No. I put a brown rinse through my hair. I thought the hairstyle—"

"And the glasses?"

She'd brought them along from a Hollywood-studio props department. "You have something against women who wear glasses?" she asked sardonically.

"Not when they need them." He removed the glasses, tested them out and tossed them on a wobbly wooden table strewn with old hunting and travel magazines. Next, he turned his attention to her attire, giving the drab gray business suit and prissy white silk blouse with a ruffled collar a quick scan. In her real life, Rebecca wouldn't have been caught dead in something so unflattering. She glared at him as he finished his inspection.

Being beautiful, Zach decided, was only half of the actress's problem—and his. It was the willful, determined glint in those delicious brown eyes that was the real kicker. Something told him that his plan to give the movie star a few quick pointers and then send her merrily on her way back to La La Land, might not pan out.

"Tomorrow wear jeans. And a sweatshirt. This is a dirty job." His eyes shot down to her feet. She was wearing pumps with low heels. High enough, however, to make them just about the same height. "And sneakers." Zach figured he could use every little edge he could get.

Rebecca was thrown by her first encounter with

Zachary Chapin. Even though she'd done her homework on the man, including checking out some photos and newspaper clippings, in person, the celebrated arson investigator made a disturbingly striking impression. It wasn't that he was so ruggedly handsome in a sexy, hard-edged way that concerned her. She'd dealt with plenty of actors who were just as tough looking and macho. What disconcerted her about Chapin was the jaded look in his hazel eyes, the guarded way he held himself, the wary set of his jaw as he observed her with about as much enthusiasm as a blind person at an art museum.

Okay, she told herself. *You're used to men falling over themselves when they meet you. So, this guy isn't following the pattern. Clearly a man cut from a different cloth. This makes it all the more interesting*, she decided.

"Sweats, jeans, sneakers. Fine," she said in a determinedly "cooperative" voice. "You're the boss. I'm just here to soak up the essence of the arson-squad experience. I want to learn everything about what you do, how you work, what investigative methods you favor. I want to get right down to the basics, Zach. Get at what drives you, what scares you, what moves you."

"Is that all?"

Rebecca blushed. "Within limits, of course."

He laughed dryly. "Of course," he said, grabbing his leather jacket off a coat hook and heading for the door with a quick wave to the receptionist who gave him a bare nod before gathering up some papers and heading for the inner office.

Rebecca grabbed her coat and hurried after him. "I want to assure you, Zach, that I won't curb your style in any way. I've done some reading. I've picked up some of the lingo. I've also gotten quite a bit of info on tracking down torches from the fire commissioner."

He stopped at the door and glanced at her. "Did Fitzgerald fill you in over lunch or dinner?"

Rebecca's eyes flashed. There was no missing Zach's innuendo. Nor had he wanted her to miss it. "Over dinner. A very nice dinner at Maison Claire. Would you like to know what we each ordered? What wine we had? Or are you more interested in what we did after dinner?"

"I'm not interested in any of it," he said brusquely. "Unlike you, sweetheart, I like to mind my own business."

"Do you call your partner, Joe Kelly, sweetheart?" she asked tartly.

"Not if he wants to live a little longer," a voice shot back from the other side of the door.

Rebecca thought she detected a faint blush on Zach Chapin's cheeks beneath the two-day-old stubble, as a paunchy middle-aged man sauntered into the room. Extending his hand to Rebecca, Joe Kelly introduced himself.

Rebecca took Joe's hand gratefully. Now, this was more like it. At least someone on the squad had some manners.

"So you're the new plebe," Zach's partner said amiably. He squinted as he gave her a closer look. "Anyone ever tell you you look a little like…that actress…" He paused, frowning in Zach's direction. "Come on, Zach. What's her name?"

Rebecca held her breath. She thought she'd done so well.

Zach shrugged. "I never go to the movies."

Joe's gaze returned to Rebecca's face. She wished she was still wearing the glasses Zach had so impertinently confiscated.

Joe snapped his fingers. "I got it." He wagged a finger at her. "Julia Roberts."

"Julia…Roberts?" Rebecca quirked a smile. "Hmm."

Joe winked at Zach and headed for the inner office. Zach continued on his way out.

Rebecca caught up with him halfway down the hall. "So, where are we headed, partner?"

He glanced over at her, actually smiling for the first time. Rebecca took heart. Briefly.

"To the men's room."

REBECCA WAS LEANING against the wall in the drab green-tiled hallway as Zach stepped out of the men's room. Her arms were folded across her chest. Zach hardly glanced at her before he headed for the stairs. Gritting her teeth, she followed after him.

She was right at his heels as he entered the three-story street-level section of the shabby brick building given over to fire station 72. Off to the side of one of the shiny red fire trucks, four firemen were sitting around a rickety wooden table playing cards. They looked tired, disheveled, and a little grimy. No one looked up as Zach approached. Until they spotted Rebecca.

"Hey, Zach. What's this? A new sidekick?" Hoffman, a gray-haired fireman in jeans and a well-worn Celtics sweatshirt teased.

The youngest in the group, O'Donnell, a redheaded Irishman with a faceful of freckles, beamed a smile at her. "Say, did anyone ever tell you you look like that actress…?"

"Julia Roberts," Gonzolas, a swarthy-looking fellow with acne-scarred skin, piped in.

"Yeah," Bartelli, a large, dark-haired man who wore a shiny silver Saint Christopher medal around his neck, agreed. The quartet all smirked.

Rebecca was beginning to smell a rat. It didn't take any great investigative skills to deduce that word about her true identity had been leaked. And she had a good idea who'd spread the word. And now the good old boys of fire station 72 as well as Zach's partner had decided to poke a little fun at her at her expense. She was sure the rest of the arson squad would get in their licks, too. Well, at least she could drop the incognito bit and stop looking like a frump.

Vowing not to let any of them—especially Zach Chapin—get the best of her, Rebecca smiled seductively. "Too bad I'm not Julia or I could give you all an autograph."

"She's not my favorite actress anyway," the red-headed O'Donnell said with a youthful grin. "I'll take your autograph any time. Especially if you scrawl it across an eight-by-ten glossy of you in that great little black nightie you wore in *My Kidnapper, My Love*.

Zach poked him in the back. "You must be losing it, O'Donnell," he said straight-faced. "Miss *McBride* here is no actress. She's just your run-of-the-mill, ordinary arson-squad plebe. We wouldn't want to start giving her a swelled head now, would we?"

"No way," Hoffman said, picking at a thread on his Celtics sweatshirt.

"Absolutely right, Zach," Bartelli said, with a fake cough.

"Whatever you say," O'Donnell added earnestly.

"Wasn't wearing my glasses," Gonzolas said, pretending to search his pockets for them.

Rebecca ignored the firemen's comments, concentrating instead on all the things she was itching to say to Zachary Chapin. Not that she planned on saying them out loud, certain it would only make the smug oaf think he was winning. Well, if he thought he could provoke her into quitting being his shadow and go sulking back to Hollywood, he had another thing coming. If there was anything she wasn't, it was a quitter.

Zach lit a cigarette, ignoring the No Smoking sign on the wall facing him, pulled up a spare chair to the card table, spun it around backward, swung a leg over and sat down. Rebecca glanced around. There were no other chairs in sight. O'Donnell, the youngster who was clearly a little star struck, started to rise, until both he, Rebecca, and the others at the table saw Zach's not-so-surreptitious shake of the head.

"You boys think of anything else you can tell me about the warehouse fire yesterday morning?"

At Zach's question, the four firemen turned their full attention to the arson investigator.

"I'll tell you this, Zach. I knew it stank of arson the minute I got there," Hoffman, the old-timer, offered.

"How come?" Zach asked.

Rebecca quickly pulled out a notepad and pen from her pocketbook and began writing. Zach rolled his eyes.

"First, it was Sunday morning," Hoffman said, smoothing back his gray hair. "A deserted area. No one around."

"Wasn't there a night watchman?" Rebecca interrupted.

All eyes flicked on her, then turned to Zach. He glanced over his shoulder at Rebecca. "The night watchman called in sick."

"Sick? Doesn't that sound awfully suspicious?" Rebecca persisted.

Zach took no notice of her question, turning back to the firemen. "What happened to the sprinklers? The report says they didn't go off."

"Old. Probably been a while since they've been charged or tested," Gonzolas suggested.

Or, Zach thought, the torch fiddled with them before setting the place ablaze.

Rebecca tapped the edge of her pen on the notepad. "Isn't it possible the arsonist tampered with the sprinkler system? Better safe than sorry, right?"

Okay, Zach conceded, she wasn't a total lamebrain.

"Anyone pick up any funny smells?" he asked the firemen.

All but one of the firemen shook their heads. Zach and Rebecca both zeroed in on Bartelli, who looked to be still pondering the question as he thumbed his Saint Christopher medal.

"Well?" Rebecca said impatiently. Zach shot her one of his killing looks, but she merely smiled, pleased at how quickly she was getting into the part.

"What do you say, Bartelli?" Zach said, hardly masking his own impatience—not just with the fireman.

"I sort of smelled something," Bartelli said. "In the back of the building. I came in through the rear door. At first I had my mask on, so naturally I didn't smell anything. Once we got the fire under control, I yanked it off. Man, I hate those masks."

Zach helped him along. "You smelled something when you pulled the mask off."

"Remember that fire in the abandoned apartment house in the South End at the beginning of the week? The four alarmer?" Bartelli hesitated. "The one where that old bum bought it."

"Yeah, I remember," Zach said somberly. On that one, the torch had phoned him at the office no more than ten minutes after the decayed old building blew. The poor bum holed up in the basement never had a chance. Now it wasn't just arson. It was murder.

There was a moment of silence all around. Rebecca looked at the group of men seated around this table, feeling not just respect but awe and compassion for them. These men had to face tragedy and unspeakable horrors every day. Somehow they had to figure out a way to live through it all. Her gaze came to rest on Zach. She thought again about that young girl he had tried and failed to rescue in the burning Drake Hotel. It was awful enough to think about a fire breaking out accidentally, but to realize someone had deliberately been responsible for starting a fire—a fire in which some poor, innocent person had died—was almost too gruesome to contemplate. And yet, here she was, right in the thick of it. Suddenly, this wasn't just "research."

"I picked up the same smell there," Bartelli was saying. "Or similar."

"There was nothing in any of the reports," Zach said, his tone taking on a gruffer edge.

Bartelli shrugged. "I wasn't really sure what it was. And no one else around me seemed to pick up any smell. I always did have a sensitive schnoz."

"And a big one to boot," O'Donnell teased.

Bartelli's pals had a good laugh, but Zach didn't crack a smile. Rebecca made a note. *Lacks a sense of humor.*

"Can you describe the smell?" Zach asked, snuffing out his cigarette on the worn heel of his shoe.

"Maybe a little like...ammonia. Not ammonia exactly, but...similar."

Zach nodded slowly and then rose. "Okay, boys. Thanks." Without a glance in Rebecca's direction, he headed for the exit.

Rebecca gave the firemen a brief smile as she stuffed her notepad and pen back in her purse, and once again took off after her partner, noticing his slight limp for the first time. A souvenir of the Drake fire? She felt another flash of sympathy for the man, incorrigible as he was.

She grabbed hold of his sleeve as he got to a dented red Ford sedan decorated with a few rust spots, which was parked at the curb halfway up the street from the station house.

"Where to now?" She raised her hand before he answered. "No, don't tell me. An all-male steam bath?"

One corner of his mouth edged up slightly as he unlocked the passenger-side door and held it open for her. "My Jag is being serviced," he said facetiously.

She gave a little jump when his hand darted in under her as she started to get in. He plucked out a tissue box. "Allergies."

After he settled in behind the wheel and lit up another cigarette, Rebecca turned to him. "Do you think it was ammonia Bartelli smelled? Can you start a fire with ammonia? Is that the torch's M.O.?"

Zach revved the engine. "Forget it." He pulled out into the traffic.

"In 'Blue Fire' the arsonist started the fires with an acid substance that's used in toxic waste."

"I said, forget it."

"But we both heard—"

"You didn't hear anything."

"I don't understand."

"Good. Keep it that way. Especially," he added after a long beat, "if you're going to be having any more dinner dates with the fire commissioner."

Rebecca bristled. "It wasn't a date."

"Call it whatever you want."

"So, you don't want me telling the commissioner you were asking the firemen questions about this arsonist. Now why is that? Aren't you just doing your job?"

"Do you ever run out of questions?"

"Unless, of course, it isn't your job. You wouldn't be stepping on someone else's toes here, would you, Zach?"

"This is my case. Understand? Joe and I have been on it for two months. A fire a week. Until this last week when we got two. He's stepping things up and we've got to figure out how to get a step ahead of him before he starts leaving piles of bodies in his wake."

"The commissioner pulled you off the case because of me, didn't he? Because it's too dangerous. That's why you've been so...unenthusiastic about my presence." Talk about understatement.

He glanced over at her, a faint hint of something new in those jaded eyes. Admiration? "You're smarter than I gave you credit for."

An actual compliment. She started to smile.

"But you're still a pain in the neck."

She doused the smile. "Look, I'm on your side. Tracking down an arsonist is exactly what I want us to be doing."

"*We're* not doing anything."

"And that's exactly what I'll tell the fire commissioner. He did mention he'd call to see how we were getting along," she said pointedly.

Zach glowered at her. Blackmail. Great.

Rebecca pulled her coat closed. Between the malfunctioning car heater and the chill coming off Zach Chapin, she was beginning to feel mighty cold. "So, are we going back to the warehouse? Do you have any other clues as to how he's starting the fires? Sometimes, you have to dig right into the walls for the answer. At least, Paradisi did."

He glanced at her. "Paradisi?"

"The lead in 'Blue Fire.' I'm sort of modeling her character after you."

With a weary shake of his head he returned his gaze to the street.

"Okay, okay, I know it's only a movie. But the screenwriter happens to have once been a fireman. And he did an enormous amount of research for the script."

Zach made no response.

"Do you chatter on like this with everyone, or am I special?"

He squealed to a stop at a traffic light, rotated his head and looked Rebecca right in the eye. "You're special, all right," he griped.

"You decided this wasn't going to work out before you even met me," she countered. After a moment's hesitation, she said softly, coaxingly, "You could give me a chance."

Zach was not won over. "I don't seem to have any choice in the matter. You singled me out, sweetheart. Unless you want to change your mind...."

A provocative smile curved Rebecca's luscious lips.

"No, Zach. I don't want to change my mind. You're all that I could have hoped for. And more."

Zach muttered something under his breath. Rebecca continued smiling.

FIFTEEN SILENT MINUTES later, Zach pulled up in front of a nondescript red-brick building on one of Boston's quiet side streets.

"Where are we?" Rebecca asked, looking around curiously.

Zach opened his door. "The morgue."

Rebecca swallowed. "The…morgue?"

"Wait here," he barked. "I've got to check with the medical examiner on that crisper the boys pulled out of that abandoned building Monday night."

Rebecca shivered. *Crisper.* She knew the term from "Blue Fire." It was what the firemen and arson investigators called fire victims whose bodies had burned to a crisp. Reading it in a script was one thing…

Taking a minute to build up her courage, she threw open her door and got out. She was right behind Zach as he got to the large glass door.

"I thought I told you to wait in the car."

"How am I supposed to observe how you operate if I wait in the car? Besides, there's a morgue scene in 'Blue Fire.' You see, Paradisi has this gut instinct that—"

"Thanks. I'll wait for the movie."

"I thought you didn't go to the movies."

"I'll make an exception."

"I'm flattered," she drawled.

"You ever been to a morgue? In real life?"

"Well…no. But it's all part of the—"

"I know. The essence of being an arson investigator." He pulled open the door, waving her in first with mock gallantry. "Have it your way, sweetheart."

"Do you think you could stifle the endearments?" Rebecca said as she breezed past him, entering the morgue with Hollywood soundstage-bred bravado.

3

THE MEDICAL EXAMINER'S office, far from looking grimly sterile and morguelike, was a cheery, warmly lit room done up in Early American-style furnishings. As for the medical examiner himself, Charlie Foster turned out to be a large, affable, middle-aged man with rosy cheeks and a warm, friendly smile. When Zach introduced her as his temporary assistant, Rebecca McBride, the medical examiner seemed to take it in stride. There were no sly smirks, no jokes about "Julia Roberts." Rebecca began breathing a little easier. This little visit to the morgue was going to be a piece of cake.

"Here we are," Foster said, smiling at the two of them, but then turning sober as he opened the folder and lifted up a photograph. "Nasty piece of work. Most of the poor fellow's clothes were chewed up by the fire. No possibility of ID there."

Rebecca felt slightly queasy, but when Zach glanced over at her, she acted merely interested. Acting was her business, after all.

Zach turned back to the medical examiner. "Dental records?"

Foster shook his head. "No teeth. Unless you come up with some in the rubble."

Zach held out little hope of getting an ID on the guy. He'd be buried as a John Doe, like so many others of the city's lost souls. Still, his death might not be completely in vain if, through him, Zach could get a lead on the arsonist.

"I'm considering the possibility that the torch is starting the fires with one of the nitrites," Zach said. "Just a hunch right now. It would be nice if we could pick up any traces of the substance on the body."

"Not much of a body there to speak of," Foster mused.

Rebecca swallowed hard.

The medical examiner slapped his palm on his desktop. "If you've got time now, we can go downstairs and see what we can get. I can run a couple of preliminary tests."

Both men rose. Rebecca felt glued to her seat. Zach gave her a condescending smile. "You can wait up here, sweetheart."

Rebecca sprang to her feet. "Not a chance."

Zach gave her points for stubborn pride. The two of them had more in common than he cared to admit.

THERE WAS NOTHING CHEERY about the autopsy room, and the brightness here came from cold fluorescent lighting that glinted off the white tile walls and matching floor. There were six examining tables in the large, sterile space, three of which were empty. The other three had white sheets draped over lifeless bodies—or what was left of them.

The pungent, medicinal smell that permeated the room only aggravated the churning in Rebecca's stomach. She caught Zach watching her, certain that he expected her to either race out of the room, gagging, or faint dead on the spot. Damn the man. She'd show him. *Ready. Action. Camera rolling.*

Zach followed Foster over to the examining table containing the unidentified corpse. As the medical examiner reached out to lift off the sheet, Zach took hold of his wrist, halting the movement. Feeling guilty for goading Rebecca into witnessing what could only be described as a ghoulish sight, he turned back to her.

"Listen, kid. This isn't going to be pretty. I've seen many an investigator turn white and pass out cold."

Rebecca cleared her throat, and said, in a voice vaguely reminiscent of her own, "I can handle it." Now she wasn't only set on proving something to Zach Chapin, but to herself as well. She'd set out to *live* the role of an arson investigator. And she was going to do it. Even if it killed her!

Foster waited for Zach to give him the go-ahead.

Zach nodded.

Rebecca steeled herself.

She did go chalky white as the sheet was removed and she saw the hideous sight of the charred remains of what had once been a human being. She could suddenly taste the breakfast roll she'd eaten that morning.

Zach saw her stagger, but regain her footing. He was close enough to her so that if she started to go down he'd get to her before she hit the floor.

"Are you okay?" Foster asked her, noting her ashen complexion.

"Fine," she said hoarsely, watching with horrified fascination as the medical examiner lifted a thin, sharp knife from a tray and scraped off some burned skin from what was left of the dead man's thigh. She took a long, shuddering breath, but surprised both herself and Zach by seeing it through on two feet.

When they left the autopsy room a few minutes later, Zach was doubly disappointed. For one thing, no trace of any nitrite had shown up in Foster's preliminary tests. For another, Rebecca Fox was proving to be a tougher foe by far than he'd anticipated. Not that he didn't acknowledge that it had taken all her willpower to hang in there. Still, he had to admit to a grudging respect for the movie star. He hadn't been lying to her when he'd said that plenty of the new boys on the block had passed out the first time he'd taken them down to view a crisper.

AS THEY STEPPED OUTSIDE, Rebecca found the clean, cold December air a welcome relief from the cloying atmosphere of the morgue.

"Hungry?" Zach asked cheerily as they headed for his car.

The last thing in the world Rebecca wanted at that moment was food. No, she decided. The last thing in the world she wanted was to let Zach score any points off her.

"Sure," she said with the enthusiasm of a Sarah Bernhardt. "What do arson investigators like to eat for lunch?"

"My favorite diner just happens to be in this neck of the woods." He left her to open the passenger door for herself while he sprinted around to the driver's side.

A diner. Perfect, Rebecca thought morosely. Cigarette smoke, greasy food, a health nut's hell. Okay, she'd order a salad. Without dressing. How bad could it be?

THE RED WING DINER looked more like a shoe box than a restaurant. It was a dreary cinder-block rectangle with a metal roof, lit up by fluorescent strips. As they stepped inside, Rebecca's nose was assaulted by the smell of stale coffee and grease. A long, speckled brown Formica counter edged with worn chrome ran the width of the place, across from which was a long row of green plastic booths. Each booth sported its own wall-mounted chrome jukebox. Echoes of a twangy country-and-western tune filled the air.

Save for a couple of waitresses and the short-order cook, they were the only actual diners to be seen.

"Popular little spot," Rebecca said sardonically as they slid into a booth facing each other.

"Place usually clears out after two. Best hamburgers in town," Zach said, calling out two orders of "burgers with all the trimmings" to the buxom waitress sitting at the counter finishing up her sandwich.

"I thought a salad…" Rebecca started to say.

"Naw. The salads here are lousy," Zach said, cutting her off. "Anyway, do you think a hotshot arson investigator like Toni Parisi would eat a salad?"

"Paradisi," she corrected tartly.

He grinned.

Rebecca felt a slight tightening of her throat, an edginess. Try as she might to ignore it, Zach Chapin's grin had a certain appeal. She found herself noticing the laugh lines around his eyes. Maybe he did have a sense of humor, after all. Maybe you just had to know him well enough. Not that she would. How well could you get to know someone in three weeks? Especially when that someone wasn't exactly welcoming you into his world or his psyche with open arms.

He stopped grinning, but he continued looking at her. Really looking, this time. She should have been flattered. Instead, she was uneasy. She pretended an avid interest in the listing of tunes on the jukebox.

"You were okay back there."

Zach's remark wasn't exactly a gold-star compliment, but it was more than she'd expected from him. She found herself feeling ridiculously pleased.

Her eyes shifted from the jukebox to him, a "gotcha" smile playing on her lips. "Fooled you, didn't I?"

She had fooled him. And Zach wasn't at all sure how he felt about it. About any of it.

The waitress came over with two glasses of water. Zach gave her a cheery smile. "How ya doin', sweetheart?" There was a "saved by the bell" ring to his voice.

"How would you be doing if you had to work a double shift in this joint?" the waitress responded in a flattened voice as she shuffled off.

"Great food, terrific atmosphere, real friendly staff,"

Zach said dryly to Rebecca. "Bet you're going to miss this place when you go back to Tinseltown."

"I'm not going back for a while," she said pointedly.

"This is a real ugly business, Rebecca."

She gave him points for using her actual name. A first. Progress.

"I owe it to my audience, Zach, to give them the best performance I can," she said earnestly. "I can't do that unless I let the character get right under my skin."

Zach rolled his eyes.

"What are you so worried about?" she retorted, her tone laced with frustration. "I won't interfere in any way with your investigation. And you've already admitted I handled myself just fine back at the morgue. I'm not some wimpy dame who's going to be a drag on you, Zach. I can hold my own. You have my word that you won't have to be picking me up off the floor...."

While Rebecca was giving her little speech, the waitress shuffled back to the table with the two burgers piled high with mushrooms, cheese, onions and bacon. The smell alone nauseated Rebecca. She watched with revulsion as Zach turned his burger upside down, lifted off the bottom of his bun, and reached for the red plastic catsup container next to the green plastic mustard container. Flipping it over, he gave the bottom a few whacks and squeezed until a rush of bright red catsup spurted out over the charred meat.

Rebecca stared, fixated at the sight, images of that poor, burned body at the morgue flashing before her eyes. A pained gasp escaped her lips and then the whole room started to spin. Next thing she knew, everything went black....

SHE CAME TO AS ZACH'S car jerked to a stop in front of the swank Heritage Hotel on chic Newbury Street. She looked around, confused and disoriented.

"What happened?" she asked Zach.

"I picked you up off the floor of the diner," he answered dryly as the doorman hurried over. He glanced at the liveried man and then at the posh hotel. "It's too bad all arson investigators don't get to live in such classy digs."

She gave him a sharp look. "How'd you know I was staying here?"

He held up her hotel-room key that he'd dug out of her purse. "Investigators investigate. I owe it to my audience to be as thorough as I can," he added facetiously.

She snatched the key from his hand as the doorman opened her door. "This is only round one, Chapin."

"I don't know, sweetheart. Under the circumstances, or under the table as it were, I'd call it a KO."

Rebecca was seething as she entered the hotel.

GAIL WAS READING through a pile of faxes in the actress's lavish hotel suite when Rebecca came storming through the door.

"The man's impossible. A KO, he says. Oh, would I have loved to KO him. He doesn't know who he's dealing with. All I have to do is place a friendly call to the fire commissioner and I could have that barbarian crawling on his knees, begging forgiveness, eating right out of my hand."

Gail waited until Rebecca stopped to take a breath. "I take it you and Chapin didn't exactly hit it off." She gave Rebecca a closer inspection. "You look a little green around the gills. What happened?"

Deflated, Rebecca sank into a chair. "I fainted."

"You fainted?"

"If he just would have skipped the catsup."

Gail scratched her head. "Catsup?"

"He poured it all over his hamburger."

Gail did not appear enlightened. "You fainted because he put catsup on his hamburger."

Rebecca shut her eyes. "It was so awful, Gail. So utterly gruesome."

Gail regarded her cautiously. "Isn't this taking being a vegetarian a little far?"

"That poor man," Rebecca muttered.

"Chapin?" Gail's confusion was steadily mounting.

"He did it deliberately. To drive me away."

"Maybe he just likes hamburgers."

"I'm not talking about hamburgers," Rebecca said irritably. "I'm talking about the charred body at the morgue. He didn't think I had the stomach for it. But I showed him." Her mouth set in a grim line. "Until he ordered that damn hamburger."

Gail headed for the built-in bar. "You need a drink."

"I need to have my head examined."

Gail grinned. "That, too."

Rebecca rose. "No. No, that's just what he wants. He's so sure he's got me pegged. A spoiled, pampered, weak-kneed little princess who can't take the heat. First he thought he'd scare me off because he's on the track of a mad arsonist. Then he thinks that by taking me down to the morgue—"

Gail stopped pouring the brandy into the crystal goblet. "Hold it. What mad arsonist?"

"Chapin's hot on the trail of this torch who started by burning down a building a week. But then he stepped it up to two. And a poor, homeless man died in one of the blazes."

"That's awful."

"Tell me about it. I saw him down at the morgue."

Gail took a swallow of the brandy, poured in some more and handed the glass to Rebecca.

"Chapin picked up one lead from Bartelli."

"Who's Bartelli?" Gail poured herself her own brandy.

"A fireman. He smelled something funny when he

was putting out the blaze. Chapin thinks it might be a nitrite. Foster ran some tests, but so far..."

Gail shook her head in bemusement. "Who's Foster?"

"The medical examiner. I'll tell you something, Gail, when I wasn't too busy feeling positively ill, it was incredibly thrilling. A lot of what happens in 'Blue Fire' is happening here in real life. I really lucked out."

Gail set her glass down and took hold of Rebecca's shoulders. "Lucked out? Rebecca, think about this a minute. You're telling me that Chapin is hot on the trail of a madman arsonist and you're playacting being his sidekick. This could be dangerous. Did you ever think about that?"

"I'm not playacting, Gail. And sure, it's dangerous. That's what makes it so...powerful, so...intense. This is the real thing. I'm getting the opportunity to really eat, live, and breathe the part." She quirked a smile. "Well, maybe not eat." She glanced around her opulent suite. "But as for living the part, I have to admit Zach was right." She rubbed her hands together. "I think I can take care of that pretty easily."

As Gail heard the excitement in Rebecca's voice mount, her worry began to mount in equal proportion. Gail doubted Rebecca knew what she was getting herself into.

Rebecca sipped her brandy, her expression thoughtful. "I'll tell you something else, Gail. Chapin may be a hard-nosed bastard, but he isn't in this for the glory. And he isn't trying to prove he's tough or gutsy. It just comes naturally. Even if I can't stand the man, I have to admit he has stirred my curiosity."

Gail smiled faintly. She had a hunch that wasn't all that was getting stirred.

O'MALLEY'S BAR WAS around the corner from the bureau, a popular hangout for the arson boys and the fire fighters of station house 72. The place was dark, most of the fluorescent-light fixtures having been on the fritz ever since Zach could remember. Not much of a drinker these days anyway, Zach saw O'Malley's more as a place to unwind—the right place to be at that particular moment since he was wound up tighter than a newly coiled spring.

The bar was almost empty. Too early for the fire boys. They filled up the place just before and after a change in shifts. A few neighborhood locals occupied some of the stools at the bar. Hank, the day bartender, a brawny, middle-aged guy with a large hooked nose, gave him a bright smile.

"Say, is it really true that you're playing host to the hottest little number on the silver screen?"

Zach grimaced, regretting now that he'd blown the actress's cover. He'd thought it would drive her off. Instead, it was driving him nuts.

"She's not so little," he muttered. "Give me a beer."

"Think you could get me her autograph?" Hank asked as he filled the order. "Something like, 'To Hank, the love of my life…'"

"Sure, sure," Zach said distractedly, spotting a familiar face in one of the back booths. He took his beer and headed over there.

Joe Kelly was nursing his second beer as Zach slid into the booth across from him.

"You look as lousy as I feel," Zach said wryly.

"One day with Adams and I'm already climbing the walls," Joe grumbled about his new partner. "Everything with this guy's gotta be by the book. Do you know, he can quote chapter and verse from the manual. Must have been a star student in Sunday school."

"You think you've got it bad," Zach countered. "I'd trade places with you any day."

Joe gave him a dubious look. "Rebecca's a lot easier on the eyes. And I bet she smells better. Did you ever get a whiff of that after-shave lotion Adams soaks him-self in?"

"At least you won't have to spend your time scrap-ing Adams off the floor."

Joe peered at Zach over the rim of his beer glass. "She pass out on you? Or did you knock her out?"

"Very funny."

Joe grinned. "You aren't laughing."

"I may never laugh again," Zach said somberly.

Joe set his beer down and leaned a little closer. "So, what's the scoop, Zach? What's it like hanging out with a gorgeous, famous movie star?"

Zach's eyes narrowed to slits as he spat out, "Hell." He took a long swig of his beer and motioned to a pass-ing waitress to bring him a Scotch, straight up.

Joe's expression held a shadow of concern. "It's been a while since you ordered hard liquor, Zach." Close to three years, to be precise. After his divorce and then the Drake fire, Zach had hit the bottle pretty hard for a time. It had been Joe who'd finally convinced him he wasn't going to shake off his demons that way.

Zach sighed, recalling with a start the alcoholic haze he'd once let himself slip into. He canceled the Scotch and gave his partner a weary look. "This is crazy. What is she doing here? How did I get elected to baby-sit?"

Joe grinned. "You're the best."

"A few hours with her and I'm already thinking about getting sloshed. What condition am I going to be in after three weeks?"

"I'll say one thing. Her timing couldn't have been worse. By the way, Collins wanted me to remind you that any further communication you have with the torch gets reported on the double to either me or Ad-ams."

"Forget Adams," Zach growled. "I'm still on this case, Joe. It's still you and me."

"But—"

"We just won't be working in tandem, that's all." Zach pushed aside his beer, lit a cigarette, and filled his partner in on his conversation that morning with the firemen and his visit to the morgue.

Joe rubbed his thumb back and forth across his lips. "Amyl or betyl nitrite, huh?"

"Nothing showed up on Foster's preliminary tests, but I want to go back to each of the sites and do some more scrounging around."

"What about your new partner?" Joe asked cautiously.

"She's not my partner, she's my albatross," Zach snapped.

Joe grinned. "My Millie's nuts about her. She's seen all her movies. Flipped over that last one she did—*My Kidnapper, My Love.*" A flush rose up Joe's neck. "Gotta admit I kinda liked that one myself. Don't usually go in for that type of thing. You know me. Give me karate, kung fu, or Schwarzenegger and I'm happy. I'll say one thing about the 'Foxy lady.' She sure can act. And looks damn good while she's doing it."

Zach sat there listening with a deep scowl on his face. "Are you through? Maybe you'd like an autographed picture of her, too. 'To Joe, with all my love…'"

"Not me, but Millie would sure love an autographed photo. Not with that particular inscription…"

Zach dropped his head in his hands. "I don't believe this is happening to me."

"Actually, Millie's kinda hoping she'll get to meet her. The kids, too." Joe hesitated. "Millie…uh… suggested that maybe since Eileen won't be around for Christmas that you might…"

Zach's head shot up. He gave Joe a sharp look. "Might what? Bring her over for Christmas dinner? Forget it. Just forget it. Isn't it bad enough I've got her on my back during work hours? You think I want to spend my off-hours with her, too?"

"Take it easy. You know there are a lot of guys out there who'd give their right arm to cozy up to a sexy movie star like Rebecca Fox. And here you are bitching about it."

"So I'm not star struck. Sue me."

Joe laughed. "So forget she's a star. That's the way she wants it, anyway."

"Yeah. And she usually gets what she wants, doesn't she?" Exasperation was thick in Zach's voice.

"True enough," Joe mused, then gave his younger partner a crooked smile. "If I were you, I'd watch out in case she decides she wants you."

"She's already got me."

Joe's eyes twinkled. "I'm not talking professionally."

"Yeah, right." Zach laughed dryly. "A match made in heaven."

IT WAS CLOSE TO FOUR in the afternoon when Zach stepped out of O'Malley's. He stood there as a cold, snowy dusk descended over the city, trying to decide whether to go back to the office and tackle some dreary paperwork, or pick up a salami-and-Swiss sub with all the trimmings and head on home. His stomach growled, reminding him that he never had gotten around to having lunch that day. Rebecca had passed out cold just when he was about to bite into that juicy burger.

Reflecting on the incident reminded him of the disturbing sensations that had coursed through him back at the diner as he'd gathered the unconscious Rebecca in his arms and carried her off to his car. She'd been no lightweight package, but she'd felt distressingly good in his arms. For a few minutes, he found himself having to fight off some R-rated fantasies about her. They might even have shifted to X-rated if he hadn't fought them off so vigorously.

Zach headed across the street to the sandwich shop.

Forget the office. He would grab a sub and go home. His head was pounding. He blamed it on the beer. By the time he got to the curb on the other side of the street, he shifted the blame to Rebecca. Which only got him thinking about her again. Thinking about her ticked him off. If he was going to spend his time thinking about a woman, then he ought to be thinking about Eileen. Sweet, attractive, undemanding Eileen. Why, she even liked the Celtics. Eileen was perfect for him. The problem was, if she was so perfect, why couldn't he stop thinking about Rebecca's silky, flawless skin, the way her voluptuous body had felt in his arms...?

His features darkened. He was determined to erase his "albatross" from his mind. Maybe a salami-and-Swiss would help. He hoped the Celtics were playing that night. He could always lose himself in a good basketball game on the tube.

As luck would have it, the sandwich shop turned out to be right next door to a video-rental store. Zach groaned audibly. There she was. Right there in the window. A life-size film poster of none other than the celebrated movie star herself. *So Hot She Sizzles* was emblazoned in boldface red lettering across the top. At the bottom of the poster, also in red, was inscribed The Luscious, Irresistible Rebecca Fox Starring In *My Kidnapper, My Love*. It was what was in the middle of the poster, though, that caught Zach's full attention.

The sultry movie star herself, sprawled provocatively across a big, brass bed in all her glory, wearing a sheer black nightie, her arms pulled over her head and tied to the ornate brass headboard with a white silk scarf at her wrists. She didn't look too unhappy about it. She looked hot, sexy...irresistible. A shadowy male figure was standing at the door, staring at her. Just as Zach was staring at her.

The temperature outside must have been below freezing, but Zach was standing outside that window sweating. Fighting the rush of lust-filled fantasies swooping back into his head. And cursing himself for having them.

For a minute he was tempted to pivot around and head back to O'Malley's and have that Scotch after all. But he didn't go back to the bar. And he didn't go into the sandwich shop for the salami-and-Swiss sub. As if some force greater than himself had clicked into operation, guiding him like radar, he walked into the video store and rented their last copy of *My Kidnapper, My Love*.

It's dark, too dark to see clearly at first. Slowly, a faint light filters into the room. A bedroom. A wisp of a black nightie lies discarded on the floor beside a pair of jeans and a shirt. Two figures—a man and a woman—naked and entwined on a large brass bed, their bodies reflected in the mirrors on the wall and ceiling. Beautiful bodies—the man's sculptured muscles; the woman's sleek, shimmering, satiny flesh. Mozart's "Magic Flute" is playing softly in the background. The music mingles with the couple's labored breathing.

The man moves atop the woman. She arches, arms stretched out over her head. Her wrists are tied together and then to the headboard with a silk scarf. Her eyes are closed, her features strained. Not in pain—in passion. As she grinds up toward him, her head tilts back.

He cups her head, kissing her—hard, rough. She writhes beneath him, matching his ardor. When he releases her, her mouth moves to his shoulder—she bites. He winces just a little. He kisses her again. Harder.

"Should I let you go?" he murmurs.

"Yes," she says huskily.

"Why?"

"Because I won't leave you."

They stare into each other's eyes for several beats.

"What if the time comes that I want you to leave?"

She smiles provocatively. "Will you?"

"Yes." A beat. "No." Another beat. "You'll leave. Whether I want you to or not. Whether you want to or not."

A shadow of sorrow sweeps across her beautiful face. "Then don't let me go."

He grabs her fiercely, their eyes on each other, burning. They begin kissing greedily, his tongue in her mouth. Her wrists strain against the silken cloth keeping her bound. He strokes her full, ripe breasts....

They are melting into each other now, their bodies pressed tightly together, his hands cupping her firm, shapely buttocks, lifting her. They're devouring each other. She opens her mouth in an impassioned cry.

The music gets louder, louder....

Zach's fingers were trembling as he flicked off the television. He sank back against his couch, his own breathing labored. A bead of sweat ran across his brow. He glowered at the tube, now radiating an eerie blue light, trying to ignore the core of aching warmth uncoiling in his groin. He should have watched the Celtics. He should have done just about anything but watch that dumb movie starring the luscious, irresistible Rebecca Fox.

How was he going to face her tomorrow? He felt like some damn Peeping Tom. Okay, so it was only a movie. Okay, so the lovemaking was simulated. He wouldn't even entertain any other possibility. Still, Rebecca was naked. That part was real. Those were her full, high, voluptuous breasts. Her fine, pearly smooth, flawless buttocks. He pictured her stretched out—not on that brass bed—on his bed. Beside him. Her arms lifted. Forget the bondage. That wasn't his thing. He'd want to feel her arms circle around him, caressing his body while he ravaged hers....

She was so damn beautiful. Like he'd thought from the first—too beautiful for her own good. And his.

He ran his tongue over his dry lips. His stomach grumbled. Only then did he remember he hadn't picked up that sub. There was nothing in his fridge worth thinking about. Some moldy cheese. Stale bread. A couple of cans of beer.

The beer was tempting. Too tempting.

His eyes fell on the empty box from the video that displayed a miniature version of the poster. She looked better on the tube. Better still in real life, even "incognito." He tossed the video box across the room.

He lit his last cigarette, taking a long drag as he crumpled the empty pack. The thing to do, he decided, was to get out of his apartment, buy a fresh pack of weeds, drop in at a nice little Italian trattoria over in the North End and have himself a big steaming bowl of pasta with marinara sauce.

He snapped his fingers. Even better, why not give Eileen a call and invite her to share some pasta with him? Sweet, lovely, uncomplicated Eileen. Okay, so their lovemaking had never matched anything he'd just witnessed in that stupid movie. Hell, that was pure fantasy. Movie magic. The right lighting, the right music, the right director calling all the shots.

His mind started to wander. What was it like when she was off the set? Did her body still glisten? Was the passion as intense? Did she know all the right moves? Could it be that good in real life? Better?

He cursed. He was supposed to be thinking about Eileen, not movie-star sex goddess, Rebecca Fox. He grabbed up the phone, started to dial Eileen's number.

Three digits in, he stopped abruptly, scowling. What the hell were the last four digits again? 7624? 7426? 7246?

He slammed the phone down. Not a good night for a dinner date, anyway. He'd be lousy company. He was in a rotten mood. Too on edge. Too irritable. Too damn horny. Not that Eileen might not oblige his lust. The truth was, it wasn't Eileen he wanted.

Grabbing up his coat, he strode angrily out of his apartment.

The television screen was still glowing that eerie blue tint as the door slammed shut....

4

REBECCA WAS PACKING one bag as Gail looked on disapprovingly.

"I don't get it," Gail said. "Why can't you 'experience the real-life drama' during the day, and come back to your nice, civilized hotel suite at night?"

"Just think," Rebecca said cheerily. "You can have the whole suite to yourself for the holidays. You can even throw your family a Christmas party here."

"I can just see Mom and Dad, my brother Teddy and the rest of the brood trooping into the Heritage for a holiday bash," Gail said dryly. "They've probably never even been on Newbury Street. They're simple folk."

Rebecca smiled reflectively. "Simple folk. Exactly." She smoothed back her hair. It was still damp from her shower. The brown rinse had washed out and she'd decided not to bother redoing it.

"You're not listening to me, Rebecca. The point is—"

"Say, you didn't bring along an old sweatshirt by any chance?"

Gail raised her eyes to the ceiling.

"I know," Rebecca said. "Maybe you could run out and pick up a few things for me while I finish up here."

"What things?" Gail asked warily.

"Sweatshirt, jeans, sneakers. You know the sizes. Maybe there's a secondhand store around. I'd rather everything didn't look brand spanking new."

"Rebecca..."

The phone rang. Gail picked up and then, shaking

her head, handed it over to her impossible client. "The fire commissioner," she announced.

Rebecca smiled, grabbing hold of the receiver. "Pete," she greeted him exuberantly. "It's so sweet of you to call back so quickly. Were you able to arrange something?"

As she listened to his reply, she winked at Gail. "That's terrific. Perfect."

She was still looking at her manager, gesturing toward the door. "No, tonight would be perfect. You're sure, now? Pete, I can't tell you..."

Reluctantly slipping on her coat, Gail didn't wait for Rebecca to finish her conversation with the fire commissioner as she headed out of the suite.

HE STOOD IN THE SHADOWS of a vacant brownstone town house slated for future renovation, mindless of the cold flecks of snow falling like dandruff on his lined navy raincoat. He pulled the collar up and pulled his black knitted cap lower on his head, not because he was chilled, but merely to blend in more with the darkness.

A woman walked out of a corner bar and grill, briefly clinging to the wall for support. Staggering drunk, but not a bad looker. Thirty-five, maybe forty. Could be a pro. Or just a lonely nurse or secretary with too much time on her hands. Another night and he might have ambled right on up to her, saying just enough to get the point across—he never had learned the art of sweet talk. He would use his favorite line, though. His one big come-on. He'd tell her he was a fireman. Women were always hot for fire fighters. A bleak smile cut across his gaunt, sallow face.

The door to the five-story faded yellow-brick apartment building opened and he instantly forgot all about the drunken woman. The smile on his face winked out, his mouth taking on a new, grimmer aspect as he watched Zach Chapin step out into the street, pausing to zip up his leather bombardier jacket.

Where the hell was he off to? A visit to his twit of a girlfriend over in Beacon Hill? An overnight visit? His hand slipped into his coat pocket, closed around the monogrammed lighter. He could feel the warmth spreading through him, already feel the blaze. Frustration pumped in his lungs. But he'd have to be patient. He felt lucky tonight. Maybe Chapin would be back before too long.

He watched the battered Ford pull out into the street, its headlights capturing the drunken woman for a moment as she was turning right around the corner. For a minute or two, he contemplated going after her. The two of them could generate some heat, all right. Only that kind of heat wouldn't satisfy him nearly as much or as long as the kind of heat he had in mind for that evening.

As he was pulling out a pint-size bottle of vodka from his inside coat pocket, he saw a cab pull up in front of Chapin's building. A woman stepped out, hesitating on the sidewalk, looking up at the place, then glancing around. A streetlight fell on her, so he got himself a brief look, not too brief to have any trouble seeing that this dame was a real knockout. She was wearing tight-fitting jeans and a snug peppermint-green parka, no hat, her fiery auburn hair falling in sexy waves down to her shoulders. He'd always been a sucker for redheads.

Who was she? A new tenant? He didn't think so from the hesitant way she approached the building. A visitor, then. His guess was confirmed when he saw her checking out the apartment listings in the vestibule. He wondered if she were a high-priced hooker. Too rich for his blood. Damn tempting, though. Maybe she'd take a check. He grinned.

A minute later he ambled across the street, curious to

get a closer look at her. He saw her through the building's glass door pressing a buzzer to one of the apartments. A minute passed. No response. She tried again. Still nothing. When she looked out into the street, he turned his back to her, pretending to hunt for a cab.

He expected her to come out. When she didn't, he turned back to see a short, plump man in coveralls whom he recognized as the superintendent opening the inside door, having a brief conversation with her. Then he was pulling the door to the inner lobby open, gesturing to her to step inside as if she was royalty.

He ambled back across the street, settling into his shadowy waiting spot, his eyes traveling up four stories to the corner apartment where in one of the windows the blue glow of a television was reflected. When a light flashed on in that room, he gave a start.

So, Chapin was two-timing his prissy girlfriend with a hot new number. Now he was sure Zach would be back before too long.

As THE SUPERINTENDENT unlocked Zach's door for Rebecca she gave him a warm smile. The man's lined pudgy face lit up.

"And to think he never said a word. Not one word. Wait until I tell the wife that we've got a tenant in this building who's the cousin of one of the biggest movie stars out there in Hollywood. She's gonna die when she comes back from her bingo and I tell her. I'm tellin' ya, she's just gonna die...."

Rebecca gave him a conspiratorial look. "I'm here sort of...incognito, Gus. You know how the paparazzi are. My cousin's a very private man. He'd be real upset if hordes of photographers started hanging around."

The superintendent raised his hand up, Boy Scout fashion. "I understand completely, Miss Fox. Completely. One thing I can say about my Harriet. She isn't a blabbermouth. We won't breathe a word."

"Thanks, Gus. You tell Harriet that I'll try to stop down at your place before I leave and say hi."

The superintendent's mouth dropped open. He was speechless. Rebecca smiled and shut the door, flicking on the light switch and setting down her suitcase.

So this was how a real arson investigator lived, she thought, surveying the small, but surprisingly tidy living room. Her gaze fell first on the twenty-one-inch television set sitting on top of a simulated-wood stand. The screen was glowing blue. She saw that the VCR on the lower shelf of the stand was on. She started to cross over to it, accidentally stepping on what turned out to be an empty video box.

As she bent to pick it up and saw what it was, a big smile curved her lips. So, Zach Chapin didn't go to the movies. He apparently waited until they came out on videotape.

Still smiling, she popped the video out of the VCR and slipped it back into the box, wondering what Zach had thought of the movie the critics had called her steamiest, most tempestuous work to date.

As she slipped off her parka, she continued her survey of the oblong-shaped room. The furnishings reminded her of something one could find in a Sears Roebuck catalog. A matching blue-and-brown tweed couch and love seat placed catercorner, a set of pine tables, one on either end of the couch, one larger one, resting on an Early American oval rag rug, in the center. The coffee table was empty, even of dust. A brass-based lamp decorated one of the end tables, a telephone and answering machine the other. Tidy *and* clean. Surprise, surprise. She'd expected clutter, cobwebs, maybe a couple of *Playboy* magazines strewn around, a movie-set fantasy of a working-man's bachelor pad.

Strolling into the tiny kitchen, she deposited her parka on a straight-backed chair near the door. Part of a two-chairs-and-matching-table breakfast set. Like the living room, the kitchen was also tidy. No dirty dishes piled in the sink. No open cans of cat food. No cat. Unless it was shy. She opened up the fridge, made a face. No wonder there were no dirty dishes. There was no food. None fit to eat, anyway. She was hungry, too. Not only had she skipped lunch thanks to blacking out so dramatically, she'd been too busy getting ready for her "new life" to find time for dinner. After a check of the cupboards she settled on a bag of pretzels, plucking one of the two beers from the fridge.

She was back in the living room heading for a gander at Zach's bedroom when the phone rang. After two rings, Zach's voice clicked on. "I'm out. Leave a message and I'll get back to you." Rebecca felt an odd little thrill at the sound of his deep, edging-on-surly baritone.

After the traditional beep, a female voice came on, speaking in a carefully modulated, but nervous, halting voice. "Zach, it's…me. Eileen. Listen, Zach. I know getting this message off an answering machine isn't exactly going to thrill you, but… I think we should end it, Zach. We're not going anywhere. And I… I need someone who… Well, we've been through all this before. I'm heading for Milwaukee tomorrow. Merry Christmas, Zach. Happy New Year. I mean that. I hope you find… Well, just take care. Bye."

Rebecca felt awkward and uncomfortable about having been privy to what was certainly meant to be a private message. She also felt a wave of sadness for Zach. How would he take being dumped? How much did he care for this Eileen? More than she apparently cared for him, since she was the one breaking it off.

A renegade thought pushed its way to the surface of Rebecca's mind. This meant Zach was now…unattached. Available. She quickly chastised herself for even having the thought, much less allowing herself to consider what it had to do with her. She vehemently told herself she had no interest in Zach Chapin other than as a means to an end—the end being landing the primo role of Toni Paradisi. She certainly wasn't attracted to him. He was ill-mannered, ill-tempered, ill-bred. And even if there was a smattering of attraction, she quickly chalked it up to her habit of romanticizing dangerous, reckless figures. As for Zach being a dangerous, reckless figure, of that Rebecca had little doubt.

Sorely regretting her impulsive visit, she decided to leave before Zach returned. Not only was she no longer feeling ready for a face-to-face encounter with the surly arson investigator on his home turf, she certainly didn't want to be present when he played back his phone messages, especially that last humdinger. She hurried into the kitchen for her parka, but as she stepped back into the living room, the front door of Zach's apartment opened.

The bag of groceries nearly slipped out of Zach's hands when he saw her. "What the hell—?"

"Hi," she said inanely, her cheeks flushed.

"How did you...?"

"Gus."

Stunned and shaken by her presence, he gave her a blank look. "Who the hell is Gus?"

"The superintendent. He...recognized me. I told him I was...your cousin."

Zach stared at her, speechless, his eyes darkening.

Rebecca quickly shifted her focus to the grocery bag in his arms. "Anything edible in there? Preferably not of the carnivore family? I'm starving."

"What's going on?" Zach's voice held a faltering note. Seeing Rebecca Fox in the flesh so soon after having seen her in all her glory on the tube shook him to the core—and sent a piercing flash of arousal coursing through him. He felt like he was staring into the biggest blazing inferno he'd seen in a month of Sundays. Had any woman ever looked so enticing in a pair of old jeans, a worn Red Sox sweatshirt, and sneakers? His eyes fell on her shimmering natural auburn hair. She was wearing it loose and sexy, just like in the video.

The video!

Zach's eyes shot to the TV. There, sitting on top of the set was the video snug in its box. An embarrassed flush of heat spread through him. Caught in the act. Caught with his hand in the cookie jar. He couldn't meet the sultry actress's eyes.

"What did you think?" she asked after a long, disquieting silence.

He slammed the still-open door shut with the back of his foot. "About what?" he asked in a surly voice that he hoped camouflaged his embarrassment.

"The movie."

What would she think if he told her the truth? That watching her make love to some dumb actor had turned him on. Turned him on so damn much that instead of going over to that trattoria for a bowl of pasta, he'd picked up some fast food and was going to settle down with a couple of tacos, tortilla chips and fries in front of the tube and see a rerun of *My Kidnapper, My Love.*

"Not my kind of flick. I just watched the first few minutes," was the lie he told as he set the bag down on the pine coffee table and shrugged out of his jacket, tossing it over the arm of the couch.

Another long, awkward silence ensued.

Rebecca broke it. "I checked out of the Heritage. You were right, Zach. I should live like an arson investigator."

Zach's hand was pulling out a paper-wrapped taco from the bag. It dropped out of his hand as he looked over at her with alarm. Out of the corner of his eye he spotted her suitcase over near the door.

"What?" So, that's why she was here? She'd decided

to move right in with him? Nothing doing. This was going over and beyond the call of duty. Even if the mayor himself issued the order, Zach wouldn't consent. Wasn't he having enough trouble?

Rebecca nonchalantly crossed the room, dropping her parka over Zach's jacket. Her eyes fell on the bag as she sniffed. "Mexican?"

"We better get a few things straight here, Miss Fox. Lay out a few ground rules. Sit down. No, don't sit down."

She smiled. "I never took you for an indecisive man, Zach," she teased.

"I don't know how Hollywood starlets' minds work, but whether or not you all think you own the world and everyone in it just because you prance around naked on the screen—" He stopped short. Too late.

"I wasn't naked until the end of the movie. I thought you only saw the first few minutes."

He squirmed. He didn't take kindly to squirming. "The first few, the last few, what difference does it make?"

She sat down, knowing better than to smile. "Actually I wasn't really naked. I wore a few strategically placed patches. And those close-up shots of my breasts, my butt..."

Zach could feel his whole face heat up.

"They weren't mine," she finished with aplomb.

He looked at her, astonished. "What?"

"I had it written into my contract that I don't do nude scenes. I'm just not comfortable rolling around naked in the hay with a crew and cameras hovering around. So, when things got down to the nitty-gritty, the camera cut to my double. You won't spread it around, will you? My fans might not appreciate knowing the truth."

Zach sat down, shaking his head. Movies. What a crazy business. So, he'd spent the last couple of hours having fantasies of some other woman's breasts, some other woman's ass....

He pulled out one of the tacos and a large, greasy package of fries from the bag.

"Want a beer?" Rebecca asked insouciantly. "I started one, but there's one more left."

His expression could have put icicles on a Caribbean palm tree. "Made yourself right at home, didn't you? Think you can just waltz right in and settle down. Well, let me tell you something, Miss Fox. You aren't camping out here for the next three weeks so you 'can live the part.' For one thing, I don't take very kindly to uninvited houseguests. For another thing, I happen to have a girlfriend. A very jealous girlfriend. And she wouldn't take too kindly to my having a temporary...roommate."

"Eileen?"

Zach did a double take.

Now it was Rebecca who couldn't quite meet Zach's stunned gaze. "She...called while you were out."

"You spoke to Eileen?" His voice was dazed.

"No, of course not," Rebecca said, affronted. "I wouldn't dream of answering your phone, Zach. Despite what you think... Well, you've got it all wrong. If you'd just give me a minute to explain—"

"How do you know she called?"

Rebecca sighed wearily. "She left a message on your machine."

Zach started to reach over to the answering machine.

"You might want to wait to listen until..."

Too late. He pressed the message button and Eileen's voice flicked on.

They sat there on the couch, very still, listening, both of them staring down at the rag rug at their feet. When the message switched off, there was absolute silence. Rebecca snuck a surreptitious look over at Zach. His face was expressionless, unreadable. If he was heart-broken, he wasn't about to let on.

After a couple of frozen minutes Zach unwrapped his taco and slid the French fries across the coffee table toward Rebecca. "Last I heard, potatoes weren't in the carnivore family," he said in a flattened tone. He lifted the taco and took a large bite.

At a loss for words for once, Rebecca retrieved a lukewarm, grease-sogged fry, gave it a brief, rueful examination, and popped it into her mouth.

They ate in silence for several minutes. Then Zach got up and brought back the two beers, handing Rebecca the one she'd started earlier.

"I'm sorry, Zach," she said softly.

"I can always buy more beers."

Rebecca gave him an impatient look. "Damn it, Zach. Why don't you call her back? I know she said it was over, but she didn't sound like she really wanted it to be over. Maybe she just wants some kind of a sign from you. Women who get involved with strong, silent types don't have it easy. They never know where they stand. They never know what's going on behind that strong, stoic, tough-as-nails facade you men are always wearing. She's not leaving until tomorrow. I'll bet, if you used a little charm and persuasion, you could get her to postpone her trip to Milwaukee. Give an inch, Zach. It could go a long way."

There wasn't so much as a flicker of response from Zach.

Rebecca raised her hands in frustration. "You're embarrassed, right? You don't want to beg. No, a super-hero guy like Zach Chapin, arson investigator extraordinaire, would see calling back his girl and asking for a second chance as crawling on his knees. And you were worried about me getting a swelled head. Your head is so filled with pride you probably can't find a fire hel-

met in town to fit you." The more she lectured him, the
more fired up she got.

"Not to mention conceit. I have never met a more arrogant man, and I've seen plenty of your type in Hollywood."

Her throat parched, she chugged down a few swal-
lows of beer, then leveled her gaze at him again. "Did
you actually think I would even consider for one minute moving in here with you? I'd rather live in a shelter
for the homeless than be your 'temporary roommate.'
When's the last time you looked in your refrigerator?
When's the last time you bought a fresh vegetable or a
piece of real fruit?"

She gave the Mexican take-out a grim shake of her
head. "You have lousy eating habits, Chapin. Too
much meat. Too much junk food. I bet you don't even
take a daily vitamin supplement. And another thing.
You smoke like a chimney. You're polluting your body,
polluting the air around you. You may know all there is
to know about fires, buddy, but you don't know the
first thing about health or nutrition. Eating right and
stopping smoking might even improve your disposi-
tion."

Zach took in Rebecca's long diatribe without saying a
word, or even raising a brow.

"Aren't you going to say anything?" she demanded.

"Is this why you seduced the super into letting you
into my apartment? To read me the riot act?"

Rebecca glared at him. "I didn't seduce the super.
When I saw you weren't home, I thought I could leave
a message on your door. I suppose I got a little carried
away, telling him you were my cousin, but it was the
first thing that came to my mind. And then he recognized me, insisted on letting me in to wait for you."

She pursed her lips. "Okay, I admit I was curious to
see how you lived. Nothing...personal. Strictly research. I was only here a few minutes."

"Long enough to find out about my eating habits, my love life—"

"Not to mention your viewing habits," she couldn't help teasing.

She was one step over the line, she saw from his grim expression.

"So, what was the note going to say?" he asked churlishly.

"That I'm moving in with the Kellys." She checked her watch and started to rise. "I should be getting over—"

Zach's hand shot out and grabbed her arm roughly, pulling her back down on the couch. "The Kellys? You don't mean Joe Kelly? You don't mean you're moving in with my partner."

"He isn't your partner at the moment," she reminded him.

"I saw Joe a few hours ago. He didn't say one word—"

"He didn't know. Fitzgerald spoke to Joe's wife early this evening. She was thrilled, said her kids wouldn't mind doubling up for a few weeks so I could have one of the bedrooms."

"What about Joe? Was he thrilled, too?"

"I gather he didn't mind," she said testily. "Will you please let go of my arm now? I'm just as eager to be on my way, thank you, as you are to see me go." What she didn't say was that his rough touch was having a disquietingly erotic effect on her. She sensed that Zach, so strong, so in control on the surface, had extravagant depths of passion locked away inside—passion that could blaze like tracer bullets in the night if ignited.

He released his grip on her, sharing her feeling of arousal. "You're really something." Another of his ambivalently tossed compliments.

Rebecca reached up and smoothed back her hair with both hands, her arms lifted. For a flash, Zach pictured her as she'd been in that movie, arms stretched out on the bed…showing off that satiny flesh. Okay, some of it wasn't hers. Or so she said. But some of it was.

He coughed to clear his throat. "I don't like it, Rebecca. I don't like it one bit."

She let her arms drop, her expression puzzled. "What don't you like?"

More things than he could name. Or, more to the point, *would* name. Okay, so she'd been right about one thing. He had his pride. He was certainly not about to tell her he didn't like what she was doing to him, how she was making him feel, the fantasies she kept provoking.

"I don't like you moving in with the Kellys."

"Why is that?" she prodded, arms folded across her chest.

Zach didn't fail to notice that the gesture pushed her breasts up. He could see the firm, alluring swell beneath her Red Sox sweatshirt, and found himself imagining what it might be like to slip his hands under that shirt, cupping her breasts in his large hands….

"If you think about it for a minute, Zach, it could be a good move for both of us."

His astonished expression baffled her. She didn't know they'd gotten their wires crossed.

"I mean," she went on, "I could be a kind of go-between. You can't work directly with Joe on the arson case, or your boss and Fitzgerald will bust a gut, but if you come up with something or Joe does…well, then the two of you could pass it on to me and I could—"

"No. Forget it. I don't want you in the middle of this thing." Zach got to his feet, moving away from the couch, gaining some much-needed distance from Rebecca. Even her orchidy scent, which he couldn't help breathing in, was causing him distress. And she thought smoking was hazardous to his health.

"No. Forget it," he repeated, as much to clear his

head of his traitorously erotic thoughts as for emphasis. "I've been giving it a lot of thought, Rebecca. My boss, Mike Collins, was right. It might be a good idea for me to go off the case for a few weeks, have someone else come in with a fresh view, that kind of thing."

Rebecca rose, too, walking over to him.

So much for keeping her at a distance. Zach had to stand his ground. He wasn't about to give away that he couldn't handle the proximity. That damn pride again.

"You're full of it, Zach. Do you honestly think I can't see through you?"

He certainly hoped so, or she just might slap his face.

She wagged a finger at him. "You aren't giving up this case. And even if I fall into a dead faint once a day—twice a day—I'm not giving it up, either. We're in this together. All three of us. You, me, and Joe."

He wagged a finger right back at her. "You're not in anything. You don't have the faintest idea what's going on. All you know about is memorizing lines, looking good in front of a camera, wiggling your ass—"

He got the slap he felt he had coming to him. No movie-set slap, either. This one landed on its mark, with impact hard enough to sting.

"I already told you. It wasn't my ass," she hissed, unrepentant.

Instinctively, he rubbed the palm of his hand where hers had struck. "Okay, so I got some of it wrong," he conceded dryly.

"You know as much about treating women as you know about good nutrition. No wonder Eileen—" She stopped herself from going on. *Let's keep this on a strictly professional note,* she told herself. *Let's not get personal.*

Too late.

Zach went on the attack, practically nose-to-nose with her now, forgetting the risks he was taking. He always did forget the risks when he was fired up.

"Right," he charged. "You listen to one twenty-second phone message and you think you know all there is to know about me and Eileen. You know just what a saint she is, what a bastard I am. You know that she gave it her best, I didn't give it the time of day. You know that she put her heart and soul into it and I just breezed along. You know she was all sweetness and light, and I was the one who was gruff and withholding. You know all that, don't you?" He gave her a dark, challenging look, not backing off even an inch.

Rebecca didn't back off, either. Or back down. "So, which part do I have wrong?"

Zach stared at her. He felt good and captured. The crazy thing was, he wasn't minding. A sudden disarming smile spread across his face. "None of it."

Rebecca would have been on safe ground if it hadn't been for that smile. It was one of those real million-dollar, grab-your-heart-by-the-throat kinds of smiles. She felt suddenly giddy. Before she knew she was moving, she was leaning into him.

"You think you're so tough," she murmured, her eyes on his. "I bet you'd run into a burning apartment to rescue a bowl of goldfish."

She thought his smile broadened, but she couldn't tell for sure because his smiling mouth was covering hers. He kissed better than she'd imagined. And she'd imagined the kiss ever since she'd first set eyes on him. There was heat and fire in his kiss. Passion and frustration. Ferocity and tenderness. A man truly at odds with himself. But there was no denying the hunger or the need—in either one of them.

Rebecca knew where that hot, hungry, feeling-packed kiss was leading. Straight into Zach Chapin's bedroom. What she didn't know was whether Zach saw taking her to bed as a convenient way of getting her out of his hair. Did he think once he'd made love to her, he could apply some crafty persuasiveness to get her to give up playing arson investigator? Not being

sure of the answer to that question wasn't the only reason she drew away from him, but it was the primary
one. And it wasn't easy in any case.

"Like I said, the Kellys are expecting me." She took
one or two trembling breaths, but told herself she was
under control. "So, I'll drive in with Joe tomorrow
morning. See you...at the office."

She started for the door, slipping on her parka. Zach
didn't make a move to stop her. His own breathing was
less than steady. He kept trying to figure out who had
made the first move. As if that really mattered. All that
mattered was that he was fully aware that this encounter was more dangerous than any of the burning buildings he'd gone charging into over the years. Dangerous
because Rebecca Fox not only had his number, but was
causing havoc in his carefully ordered life. After his
marriage had fallen apart, Zach had tossed overboard
all his naive fantasies about love everlasting. He'd
turned off that part of his life with a fiercely determined
twist of the tap. Now, he was hearing a disquieting
drip, drip, drip....

Rebecca paused at the door to zip up her parka,
knowing damn well that she was giving him one last
chance to tell her not to leave.

He didn't say a word, but the phone rang just as she
was reaching for her suitcase. They both looked at the
phone. Eileen?

Zach picked up. Even before he said anything, he
heard a now familiar, spine-chilling laugh.

"Things getting pretty hot up there, pal? Your new
girlfriend's a real looker. You're a lucky man, Zach. I
sure hope you appreciate that."

Rebecca was about to slip out the door, but the stark
expression on Zach's face stopped her cold, a gut feeling telling her it wasn't Eileen on the other end of the
line.

"Isn't this getting a little childish?" Zach said evenly. "Isn't it time we got together face-to-face?"

The laugh turned into a diabolical chortle. "Well, Zach, old friend, just so you don't start feeling sorry for me, I thought I'd give you a ring to let you know things are getting pretty hot over here, too."

"Where's here?" Zach said grimly, plucking out a newly opened pack of Camel cigarettes from his shirt pocket, tapping one out. He felt around his pockets for a match, coming up empty-handed.

Rebecca spied a book of matches on a small table near the door. She picked it up and crossed the room, striking a match for him, silently asking the Surgeon General for forgiveness. The cigarette lit, Zach took in a long, grateful drag, not meeting her eyes.

"You still there, Zach, old pal?"

"I'm here."

"Tell your new girlfriend to have a look-see out the window."

Close enough to Zach to hear the deep basso voice on the other end of the line, Rebecca's eyes quickly shot to the pair of windows at the far end of the room. She hurried over. Zach followed, his caller having hung up right after issuing his order.

Rebecca stared into the dark street, surveying the buildings. "I don't see anything."

Zach's gaze focused on the brownstone town house slated for renovation across the street. Just the kind of target his torch favored. Luckily, there were narrow, empty lots on either side of the building. If it went, at least it wouldn't take the rest of the street with it.

At first he didn't see anything unusual. Then, all of a sudden, there was an eerie 'popping' sound and a boarded-up window on the top floor of the five-story building exploded, spewing wooden slats and glass all over the street, along with a long lick of fire.

Rebecca, too stunned by the sight to cry out, stared

out the window, fixated. Zach had to shake her out of her reverie.

"Call 911. Now. Then get on the phone to Kelly."

He was on his way out the door when Rebecca got to the phone. She could hear the commotion in the hall—neighbors who'd heard or witnessed the explosion from their apartments. Her fingers were trembling as she called the fire department, forcing her voice under control as she gave the address. Then she called Joe's number. Millie came on.

"Tell Joe to get down to Zach's place," Rebecca said without preamble. "Fast. The building across from Zach's was just torched."

Coatless, Rebecca raced out of the building after Zach, catching up with him on the street. She started to tell him that the fire trucks were on the way, but her gaze was fixed on the burning building where something caught her eye. One floor below where the fire was already raging. A face in a window not completely boarded up. A kid's face.

Rebecca screamed to Zach, "There's somebody in there." She pointed to the window.

Zach saw. He went cold and hot inside at the same time. Sensations, but no feelings. Not now. No time. Later...

"Stay put," he barked at Rebecca. "Keep everyone back and wait for the fire trucks."

Only as Zach issued the order did she even notice that a crowd was gathering, people filtering out of Zach's building and the neighboring apartment houses, many of them in robes and slippers, huddling together, shivering with cold.

Behind her, Rebecca heard a woman say to a man, "He's crazy to go in there. He'll get himself killed."

Rebecca whirled around and glared at the woman. "No, he won't. He's a fireman." As if firemen—past or present—were somehow invincible.

In the end, Rebecca herself wasn't convinced. Where was Zach already? How long did it take to race up four flights of stairs, snatch up a child and race back down and out of the building?

Minutes ticked off. In the distance she could hear the sound of fire engines. She guessed it would still be several minutes more before they'd arrive on the scene.

Precious minutes. A lifetime. The fire crackled and raged, spreading. Flames poured from the window frames all across the fifth floor. Then more and more shooting licks. They rolled out the windows, then sizzled up to the roof in awesome waves. Rebecca was terrified that any minute now the fire would begin to work its way down to the floors below as well as up to the roof.

Seconds later, her worst fears were realized. She saw an amber glow in the window where she'd spied the child. The fire had progressed down to the fourth floor. If Zach was still up there...

She couldn't stand it any longer. She had to go in there and see if he needed help. As she started to dart across the street toward the burning building, she heard the same woman saying, "What? Is she a fireman, too?"

5

HIS ARM AND SHOULDER were throbbing from his having used his whole right side as a battering ram to force open the locked front door of the building. Zach ignored the pain as he raced across the vestibule, dimly lit by an outside streetlight. By the time he got to the stairwell, he was in the pitch black.

Grabbing onto the banister, he made his way up, two, three steps at a time. His bum leg slowed him down a little, and he was breathing heavily by the time he made it up to the third-floor landing. One more flight to go. He really should give up smoking, he told himself, as he made his way more gingerly up the next flight.

He moved cautiously now, knowing it was only a matter of minutes, maybe seconds before the ceiling rafters above him succumbed to the fire and came showering down, bringing hell and damnation with them.

He prayed a ladder company would come in fast. Here he was, going in for a rescue with no apparatus—no hose, no safety belt, no light, no smoke mask, no aerial ladder rigged up outside for a quick escape. All he had was a wing and a prayer.

"Hey, kid," he called out in the dark as he got to the fourth floor. His hoarse, breathless voice echoed off the crumpling plaster walls, the thick, pungent smoke curling around him. "Stay put and keep low to the ground. I'm coming to get you. You're gonna be okay."

Zach sounded a lot more confident than he felt. His

mind began flashing back to another time so much like this one, three years back. Hadn't he called out the very same thing to that young girl? He could still picture every single move he'd made, bursting into the hotel room that was already in flames, grabbing the slender girl off the bed, thinking she couldn't have been more than sixteen as he heaved her limp body into his arms, dashing out with her. As they descended the stairs, the flames lapped at them from above. There was no choice, no place to go but down, nothing to do but hope they would beat the fire nipping at their heels. The girl was barely breathing. She was unconscious. Maybe she wouldn't have made it even if nothing else had gone wrong. One thing about a fire, though. It was never wholly predictable. In a grotesque flash of anguish, Zach realized that an offshoot of the blaze had engulfed the vertical wooden supports of the staircase. It was diabolical. He was trapped in no-man's-land, since there was no turning back. All he could do was pray that the staircase would hold out until they made it to the bottom.

Even now, he could still feel the impact of the fall as the staircase caved in only two flights up from safety. He could still remember how he'd managed to cushion the girl against his body so she wouldn't bear any of the brunt of the landing. He could still remember the way his body thudded against the ground like a deadweight. He could still remember the excruciating pain. But, most vivid of all, was his memory of that girl's lifeless body as a fireman—a rookie, from the look of him—gently lifted her off him, shaking his head sadly....

Stop, Zach ordered himself sharply, sweat saturating his body. *Don't think about that now. Don't think about anything or anyone but this one kid.*

God, he hoped there was only the one kid. And that he was still alive.

ODDLY ENOUGH, once Rebecca stepped inside the vestibule, the awful crackle of burning timber she'd heard so clearly on the street was now muted. There wasn't even any smoke in the dank entryway. For a moment, she had the illusion she was in the wrong building.

Gingerly she crossed to the narrow stairwell. It got darker and darker the closer she came to it. It was just about pitch-black when she got to the bottom step. From here, she could pick up the acrid smell of smoke, the hiss of the fire.

In the dark, her hand searched and found the banister. She gripped it tightly. "Zach," she called out in a quavery voice.

There was no response.

Rebecca's heart lurched. She started up the first flight. When she got to the landing, the smell of smoke was more intense, the snap, crackle, pop of the blaze undeniable.

"Zach? Zach, can you hear me?"

Her heart was racing now, her body dripping perspiration. Every ounce of common sense she had told her this was madness; that she should turn back; that she could end up getting herself seriously hurt. Or worse.

Still, she began climbing to the second landing, telling herself if she got no response from Zach when she got there, she would get out herself before it was too late.

A BURNING TIMBER gave way along with a huge chunk of ceiling right in front of Zach when he was halfway down the hallway on the fourth floor. He could hear the sound of a child whimpering in the distance. "Take it easy, now. Don't be scared. I'm almost there," he soothed.

The only good thing about that burning rafter was that the fire provided some much-needed light. The kid would have picked the last apartment down the hall to hole out in. Moving with lightning speed, his plan being to grab up the kid and head out a window connecting to the fire escape, Zach burst into the last apartment.

A piece of ceiling and a rafter had given way here, too, casting a sickly glow in the vacant space. A boy, no more than twelve or thirteen, was curled up in a fetal position, sobbing quietly but intensely not a yard from where the ceiling had collapsed. Only by the grace of God...

Zach dropped to his knees in front of the child, taking a moment to place a hand on his back and give the boy a comforting pat before he scooped him up in his arms.

"Are you by yourself?" Zach asked anxiously, quickly scanning the room. "Is anyone in here with you?"

The child just kept whimpering.

"Okay, okay, just shake your head or nod," Zach pleaded, making his way with the boy in his arms to the boarded window, which he deduced opened on to the fire escape.

The boy just kept on crying. And time was running out. Zach had to set him down while he pushed open the window and then pried off the boards, kicking at them with the heel of his shoe. Relief washed over him as he saw that the fire escape was still intact. What's more, he could hear the sirens drawing closer.

Zach felt his first real rush of relief. But as he bent to pick the boy back up, a smudged little hand clutched at his shirt.

"My...brother," the kid croaked hoarsely.

Zach's heart sank. "Where?"

The boy looked up at the ceiling.

"Upstairs? He's upstairs?" Zach's stomach turned. His eyes started to smart. Only partly from the smoke.

The boy nodded, then with no warning at all, he

sprang to his feet and bolted across the room for the door leading out to the hallway that was raining down chunks of flaming wood and plaster at this point.

"Jerry! Jerry!" the terrified boy was screaming in a panicky, high-pitched voice as he raced pell-mell down the hall. "Jerry!"

The boy's abrupt flight into hell took Zach completely by surprise. He went racing after him, cursing under his breath, fury and terror over all their fates washing over him in equal measure.

REBECCA REACHED THE third-floor landing, feeling like she was ascending into the mouth of the Furies. Smoke clogged her throat and stung her eyes. Looking up the staircase she could see that the floor above was radiating a surrealistic red glow. Like the magic of colored klieg lights on a movie set. Only this was no movie set. This was real life. No director was going to call out, "Cut!" There was no glamorous, no-expense-spared trailer to which she could escape. Nor was there any escaping the reality that the fire had reached the floor above her, the floor where Zach was trying to rescue some nameless kid who'd been fool enough to seek sanctuary in a boarded-up tenement. And, Rebecca realized, there might be no escape at all for her, if she didn't turn right around and race back down the three flights of stairs and out the door.

Again, she rebelled against common sense, even self-preservation, not understanding why, not wanting to question it. She started to call out Zach's name, but broke into a fit of coughing.

A wave of dizziness followed. She sank to her knees, commanding herself not to pass out now.

Thankfully, the dizziness faded after a couple of moments. She fought back a new bout of coughing as she once again called to Zach.

There was no response at first, but then Rebecca

heard a sharp cry. The next moment a figure came into view.

"Zach." Her voice was heavy with relief.

No. Not Zach, she saw through the smoke. A boy. The boy she'd seen in the window. Their eyes met for a fraction of an instant. There was absolute terror in the boy's eyes. Rebecca clutched at the banister, the boy's terror becoming her own. Where was Zach? Had something terrible happened to Zach?

She saw that the boy was about to start down the stairs toward her, but then he suddenly reversed his direction, about to climb up into the burning inferno.

"No!" she screamed, racing up the flight of stairs after him. She hadn't climbed more than a few steps when Zach popped into view, catching hold of the boy, who was now hysterically screaming, "Jerry, Jerry, Jerry!"

A new sound cut through the sizzle of the blaze. A horrible shriek. And then a figure lurched out of the flames up above and rolled down the stairs to Zach's feet.

Rebecca cried out, the first Zach realized she was there. He was both furious at her for following him into that burning inferno and relieved to have her help.

The younger boy was sobbing uncontrollably now, bending down over his brother who lay lifeless on the ground. Zach reached down and felt for a pulse, nodding soberly to Rebecca who had raced up the rest of the stairs and was putting her arms around the crying child.

"You're brother's still alive," Zach told the boy, his tone at once gruff and reassuring. "Now, pull yourself together and we're all gonna get out of here."

He scooped up the older boy—he was maybe sixteen; around the same age as that girl. Again, he forced all thoughts of her from his mind. It wasn't easy.

"You take the little one and hold on to him for dear

life," he ordered his new "partner" brusquely. "We've just got to get down four flights and we're home free."

"Right," Rebecca said with more confidence than she felt as she took firm grip of the younger boy's arm. He was still crying, but not as hysterically. And he moved compliantly after she gave him a tug.

Zach was right behind her with his charge as they headed down the stairs. Halfway down, they stopped dead in their tracks as they heard an awful explosion below.

Zach was cursing audibly now as he realized the torch must have timed a second blast to go off. Zach's guess was the basement, but it would only be a matter of moments before the blaze hit the main floor and then started climbing up. And here they were, getting sandwiched right in the middle.

Rebecca felt the young boy's whole body stiffen in panic. She wasn't exactly the picture of calm herself, but she did her best to conceal it.

"If we hurry..." she began to say, thinking the stairs were their only option.

Zach cut her off. "No, we can't chance it." He gestured toward the third-floor hallway. "This way. We'll use the fire escape."

"I'm scared," the boy cried, resisting Rebecca's yank on his arm.

"Don't be," Rebecca said as she swept him up in her arms, grateful that she'd spent all those hours over the past few years working out at a gym. She was a lot stronger than she looked.

The fire was oozing down the walls of the hallway. Zach knew that the greatest danger at this point was of the roof going, which would cause the whole building to cave in on them. He kept his knowledge to himself.

Kicking open a door to one of the apartments, Zach led the way, only to pull up short a few yards inside as a flashover occurred and everything around them burst into flame.

"Out. Fast," Zach barked. "We'll try the next one."

The boy was clutching at Rebecca now like a lifeline as the heat of the fire made breathing hard. Zach, pumped up purely on adrenaline now, refused to consider how badly off the comatose kid in his arms might be.

They made it safely through the next apartment to the fire escape. Zach stepped out first. The sirens were loud now. He estimated the first trucks were probably only a block or two away. A block or two could make all the difference.

He glanced up. Flames everywhere. The building was ripe for an early collapse. If it went, the fire escape, which was old and rickety under any circumstances, would surely give way. Even if the building hadn't been ablaze, there was some chance the fire escape might not hold up. But there was no other choice. Zach stared straight down in front of him. One of those times when you needed tunnel vision. All you could focus on was the street below and getting down to it.

Rebecca stepped out onto the fire escape with the younger boy clinging to her, too frightened and too exhausted even to whimper. Rebecca's movements were cautious as Zach told her to go down ahead of him. It didn't take an engineer to know that the fire escape wasn't exactly up to code. She gave Zach an anxious look.

"We'll make it," he said. "Trust me."

She smiled. For some crazy reason she did.

One flight down, she had pause to reconsider. Not much pause, either. The fire escape started to give way from its fastenings. One whole side of the metal structure sagged ominously. As if things weren't bad enough, one whole section of roof had collapsed and heavy smoke and fire were blowing out and up from the basement and first floor.

"Go," Zach ordered sharply as Rebecca and her charge froze in panic.

A fire truck was just pulling up to the curb. Two firemen caught sight of them and leaped off the truck, running to their aid.

It felt to Rebecca like a movie being run at slow speed, even though in reality everyone was moving fast. She could hear the fire raging, the boy's heavy breathing, their clanking footsteps on the metal stairs.

One of the firemen was about to charge up the stairs to give them a hand, but Zach warned him off. Any extra weight and it could be curtains for all of them. As they descended that last flight, the fire escape was practically dangling from the building.

With a relief unlike anything she'd ever known, Rebecca touched ground. A fireman whisked up the young boy and ran with him to the ambulance that had pulled up behind the first truck. The second fireman took the unconscious older boy from Zach. Zach couldn't meet the fireman's eyes; didn't want confirmation of something he both feared and dreaded—that this boy, like that girl three years back, hadn't made it.

Rebecca gripped Zach's hand as the paramedics administered oxygen to the boy and checked his vital signs. One of them looked up, a smile more welcome than sunshine on his face. "I think he's gonna pull through. Amazingly enough, most of the burns are superficial. Got a few bad spots on his legs and back. Biggest problem, though, is smoke inhalation."

Zach nodded. Moments later the ambulance pulled out with both boys. Only then did Zach turn to Rebecca. He gave her a haggard look, which was all he could muster at the moment. "You realize you could have got yourself killed in there?"

Suddenly, Rebecca found herself fighting back tears.

"Yes. And don't you dare give me a lecture about it now, Zach Chapin, or I... I..." She couldn't go on.

Zach pulled her into his arms and held her tight. There was nothing erotic about his embrace, or about the way Rebecca clung to him.

The firemen of engine 34 were already busy at work, trying to contain the blaze. Three of them, sporting masks, were pulling in a heavy two-and-a-half-inch hose, necessary for a body of fire of that magnitude. Several firemen were coming in from behind, sporting heavy air packs. Others were dragging in hoses on either side of the burning building. Water started gushing, steam erupting like a volcano. Meanwhile, cops from a couple of cruisers who had set up makeshift ropes to keep onlookers at a safe distance, were making sure no one crossed the line.

Rebecca heard one of the firemen shout to his crew, "The roof's about to blow. We're gonna be here awhile."

Zach drew Rebecca across the street, which had been cordoned off from all traffic.

"Go back upstairs to my place," he told her. "Take a hot shower if you want." He wondered if she even realized she was black with soot and had ash and bits of plaster sprinkled through her hair. Not that he looked much better.

"What about you?" she asked.

"I've got to stick around until the fire's out and then go in and have a look." His voice was even hoarser now, the rawness in his throat reminding him of how he used to feel after too many drinks and a thousand cigarettes. Well, at least he'd done away with one of those vices.

"I'll stay," Rebecca said, that familiar glint of determination in her eye.

Zach was going to argue, but changed his mind. Not because of the hassle he knew she'd give him, but because he figured fair was fair. He owed her that much. More. He knew there was a good chance he wouldn't have made it without her. Or either of those two kids. Damn. Now he was stuck feeling gratitude toward her on top of everything else.

Joe Kelly was on the scene minutes after the fire trucks showed up. Zach knew he must have driven like a bat out of hell because he lived at least twice the distance away as the firehouse.

Rebecca smiled weakly as he approached them. "Hi. I hope Millie isn't upset that I was…detained."

Joe gave both her and Zach a scrutinizing look. The two of them reeked of smoke; their clothes and bodies were smudged with grime and soot. He zeroed in on Zach, his expression incredulous. "You brought her in there with you?"

Zach smiled crookedly. "Not exactly." He gave his partner a brief rundown. When he finished, he said, "I want a report from the hospital on those two kids, especially the older one."

Joe nodded, his gaze shifting to the blazing building. "Any idea how it started?"

Zach glanced around before answering. "Not how, but who."

Joe gave him a sharp look. "You got another call from—?"

"You didn't hear about it until tomorrow."

"Zach…"

Rebecca, who had remained quiet during the two men's interchange, began to shiver. She took hold of Joe's arm.

"I don't suppose you could run up to Zach's apartment and get us our coats? And you might want to give your wife a call and tell her we'll probably be here through the night."

"I already told her," Joe said with a broad smile. He shrugged off his plaid wool jacket and put it around

Rebecca's shoulders. "This will keep you warm until I get back."

Joe winked at Zach before he took off.

"Will you get in trouble with your boss?" Rebecca asked Zach as they watched the fire being slowly brought under control.

"Trouble? You mean for holding back information, or for endangering the life of the fire commissioner's favorite Hollywood movie star?"

"You didn't endanger my life. I did. You leave Fitzgerald to me. I'll make sure he doesn't come down hard on you."

"Oh no. I gave up having someone else fight my battles for me when I was five."

Rebecca smiled. "Somehow I can't picture you as a five-year-old."

"The point is, you let me deal with Fitzgerald."

Her smile deepened. "If I didn't know you better, I'd think you were jealous, Chapin."

Zach was trying to think up a comeback, but was saved by Joe's reappearance on the scene. Rebecca slipped off the plaid coat and let Joe help her into her parka. Zach shrugged on his leather jacket.

The three of them stood there, along with the rest of the onlookers, watching the firemen battle the fire. Zach's gaze trailed over the small crowd. For all he knew, one of them might be the torch. He searched their faces for some clue, something that might give him away. A smirk, a shadow of a smile, a glint of madness in his eyes. Was it someone he knew? Someone who had it in for him? Had the torch spotted those two poor kids inside before he set the place off? Had he counted on Zach making a rescue attempt? Had the bastard hoped he'd fail?

Zach was distracted from his ruminations as he heard Rebecca let out a gasp of horror. The roof had caved in, the metal fire escape first dangling from the building, then collapsing to the ground like an accordion. He put a comforting arm around her, but quickly retrieved it when he caught Joe observing the gesture and smiling. The last thing he needed right now was to have his old buddy ribbing him about having a thing for some Hollywood movie star.

Did he have a thing for her?

Within a couple of hours most of the fire was out, the firemen shutting down the big lines and heading inside what was left of the burned-out building to do some interior fire fighting. They all wore gas masks.

Rebecca felt a rush of trepidation for them. And that's when it really hit home that she might not have made it out of that building alive. She swayed against Zach. Both he and Joe caught hold of her.

"Steady now," Joe soothed.

"I'm okay," she muttered, but she wasn't okay. She was feeling dizzy again. She fought it off, telling herself Zach would never let her live it down if she passed out again.

Joe ran over to one of the fire trucks and bummed a foam cup of coffee from one of the men who'd come off duty for a breather. Rebecca gave Joe a nod of thanks, offering some of it to Zach who shook his head. She drank the hot brew gratefully, curling her icy hands around the cup.

Joe sidled over to Zach's side. "Wanna tell me about the call?"

Zach's expression was grim. "Nothing much to tell." With Rebecca within earshot, he wasn't about to recount the torch's remark about him having a hot time with his new "girlfriend."

"Why you?" Rebecca broke in. "Why does he call you?"

Zach shrugged. "Maybe he read about me in the paper."

"Or maybe he knows you," Rebecca countered.

"We've gone through every torch Zach has ever brought in who might be out on the street now," Joe said. "We tracked down every possibility and came up empty-handed."

Rebecca frowned. "Couldn't it be someone who bears a grudge against you for another reason?"

Zach smirked. "Are you implying I'm not a popular guy, beloved by all?"

"Seriously, Zach..."

"We've covered that territory," Joe said as Zach walked off toward one of the trucks, muttering something about seeing if any word had come through on the teen he'd carried out of the building. Zach was also thinking about the kid brother. The kid would be bound to bear scars from the experience, too. Even if his weren't the kind that showed. Later in the day, he'd have to go over and question the kid on the chance he'd spotted the torch. And if his brother was out of the woods, he'd question him, too. Of course, if his brother didn't pull through, the younger boy wouldn't feel much like answering questions. Nor would Zach feel much like asking them.

"He must have enemies," Rebecca said to Joe when Zach was a few yards away.

Joe smiled. "Believe it or not, he is pretty well-liked. Once you get to know him."

"What about his ex-wife? Does she still like him?"

"Cheryl?" Joe laughed dryly. "No. No, she probably doesn't like him much these days. As for still loving him, though... Well, once you love the guy, it isn't easy turning it off."

Rebecca looked away uneasily. "Anyway, the torch is a guy. I heard his voice on the phone. It was very low, creepy sounding. A nut case."

"Maybe."

Rebecca looked back at Joe. "You don't think so?"

He winked as Zach strode back over. "I leave the thinking to my old buddy here."

"Thinking about what?" Zach asked gruffly.

"About what makes people tick," Joe said.

Zach gave Joe a rueful smile. "If I knew that, I'd be a shrink instead of an arson investigator."

Joe gave a chuckle, but Rebecca's expression was solemn. "Any word on the boy?"

She saw the first glimmer of a real smile on Zach's face. "They say he'll pull through."

Rebecca breathed a sigh of relief.

Zach's smile vanished. "The next kid might not be so lucky. This bastard's got to be stopped. I'm not gonna sleep nights until I track him down."

IT WAS CLOSE TO DAWN by the time what was left of the building was safe enough and cooled down enough for the makeshift arson team to enter. Joe got his tool kit out of his car, along with a trio of metal safety helmets. Zach had already tried to talk Rebecca out of going in to investigate with them—to no avail. Joe smiled to himself. The dame was not only easy on the eyes but as stubborn as all get-out. And gutsy. What a matchup she was for his old buddy.

"See here," Joe was saying to Rebecca as he pointed his flashlight on a charred piece of wall in the basement. "Less soot, more heat. That means there was a slow burn before the explosion."

Rebecca nodded, glancing over at Zach who was about five yards away, collecting charred specimens. "What's he looking for?"

"Some sign of accelerant. The starting place." They both heard Zach grumbling to himself.

Joe smiled. "He hates when you have to go looking for it."

Both men continued their investigation, Zach absolutely silent while Joe continued answering Rebecca's questions and giving her a running commentary, even though he knew it was bugging his partner.

"Joe. Come here," Zach called out. "I think this is where he set it off. If my nose isn't playing tricks on me, I think we'll find some definite traces here of a nitrite."

Joe hurried over, Rebecca at his heels. She stopped midway, something catching her eye on the ground. She bent down to pick up what she thought was a coin, but turned out to be a gold button. Scooping it up, she called out excitedly, "I think I found something, too."

Rebecca was sorely disappointed when neither arson investigator seemed convinced the button was a direct lead to the torch. Zach said distractedly, "It could have fallen off anyone's coat."

"Like who?" Rebecca persisted. "The place was boarded up. No one was living here."

"Tell that to those two boys we carted out earlier."

Joe slipped the button into a small plastic bag. "We're not saying it isn't a possible lead, honey. We'll check everything out."

"Yeah, put Adams on it," Zach said to Joe.

Joe cracked a smile, then checked his watch. "Guess what, folks. It's almost show time. I don't know about the two of you, but I'm gonna zip on back home, take a nice, hot shower, change into some clean clothes and mosey on down to the office."

Zach was still taking some last scrapings. "Right. I'll see you down there later. I want to take this stuff over to the labs, then stop down at the hospital...."

Joe gave Rebecca a questioning look.

"I've got my gear up in Zach's apartment. I might as well hang around here with him."

TWENTY MINUTES LATER, while Rebecca was showering in his bathroom, Zach was sitting at his kitchen table munching on a cold, disgusting "breakfast" taco, trying to figure out why he hadn't balked at her decision to come back up to his place instead of taking her suit-case and heading back with Joe.

When she stepped into the kitchen, wrapped in his white terry robe, smelling of Irish Spring soap, her presence hitting him like a scented, silken whip, he knew why.

6

"I COULD RUN DOWN TO the grocery store and pick up
some...regular breakfast stuff," he said awkwardly,
wondering the whole time he was talking whether or
not she was wearing anything under that robe.

"Just coffee," she said quietly.

"Instant."

"Fine."

He started to rise, but she waved him back in his seat.
"I'm a whiz at making instant coffee. Want some?"

He didn't really, but he nodded.

She filled a small saucepan with water and set it on
the stove.

"I should be plenty steamed at you for following me
into that building." Zach's voice was gruff, but it felt
forced.

She rested her hands on the edge of the stove. "I've
never done anything like that before. I never actually
saw myself as a very daring person." She turned slowly
to face him. "I was scared out of my wits."

Their eyes met. "You should have been."

She swallowed hard. "It was close, wasn't it?"

"Yeah. It was close."

She looked down at her hands. They were trembling.
She stuck them in the oversize pockets of his robe.

He rose slowly and walked over to her. "You were
real good. You stayed calm. You kept your head."

His compliment made her feel a little giddy. She
knew he wasn't the sort to dish them out frequently.

Her pleasure quickly evaporated when he grabbed

her shoulders roughly, his eyes dark and threatening. "And if you ever do such a damn foolhardy thing again, sweetheart, I'll…"

She gave him a challenging look. "You'll what?"

There was a long, strained pause. His hands were still gripping her shoulders. Her soapy scent was clouding his thoughts. His touch was clouding hers.

"I'll take you over my knee and spank you till you cry uncle, that's what," he finished, a lot less irately than he'd begun. Suddenly, the idea of taking Rebecca Fox over his knee became excruciatingly enticing, only it had nothing to do with being angry at her.

Rebecca's mind was running on the same track. "Uncle," she murmured softly, her seductive smile curling around him in a conspiratorial embrace.

He was almost a goner, but then warning sirens went off in his head. Talk about playing with fire. He instantly let go of her shoulders like he might actually get burned, shook his head and backed off, lighting a cigarette.

Zach wasn't the only one who knew they were stepping into dangerous terrain. Rebecca tried to pull herself together, telling herself that she wasn't thinking straight, and that Zach was doing her a favor by thinking rationally for both of them.

"Water's boiling," he mumbled.

Rebecca smoothed back her damp auburn hair. "So it is."

Zach got a couple of mugs down from the shelf, tapped some instant coffee in each one. Rebecca reached for the hot handle of the pot on the stove, only to jump back, crying out in pain.

Zach grabbed her hand and pulled her over to the sink, running the cold water over her palm.

Rebecca started to laugh.

"What's so funny?"

"I come out of a burning building without so much

as a scratch and go and burn my hand on a dumb pot handle."

Zach smiled. "I guess that is pretty funny."

She shut the water off with her free hand. "I'm fine."

He examined her palm closely. "I should put some first-aid cream on it."

"No, it's okay. Really."

He was still holding her wrist. He didn't think he could let go. He knew he didn't want to.

"Rebecca…" He wanted to explain how it was with him. He wanted to say that this was the last thing he needed—getting in over his head with a famous Hollywood actress. It was crazy. Nuts. Stupid. So, where were the words?

The morning sun flooded the kitchen.

Rebecca took a step closer to him.

His free hand reached out of its own volition and touched her still-damp auburn hair. Her robe had parted, revealing sumptuous cleavage. Whoever that double had been in the video, Zach decided she didn't hold a candle to the real Rebecca.

"Zach." His name came off her lips like a barely audible plea. Her heart was hammering. She was afraid he'd have some cockeyed notion that because she was a movie star, that this sort of thing happened to her a lot. She wanted to tell him it didn't. She wanted to tell him that she was very cautious when it came to intimate relationships; that they'd been few and far between. So where was all of her caution now? It seemed to have gone up in smoke.

They were so close. She could feel his warm breath fanning her face. The warmth spread over her breasts, her belly, between her thighs. Her body had never felt so sensitive.

Zach's hand tightened into a fist around her hair, forcing her to arch her head back. Her robe—his robe—

opened a little more. He untied the sash. His hands were trembling now.

Her injured palm came up to stroke his cheek, still smudged with ash. He shuddered from the fiery lick of desire the caress sparked. They'd been through hell together. From hell to heaven. It seemed only just.

Gently, he pushed the robe away from her shoulders. Nothing quite prepared him for how utterly exquisite he'd find her body. His breath caught in his throat and he could feel the muscles in his stomach contract almost painfully.

The robe slipped down her arms, falling in a puddle around her feet. The morning light glistened off her flawless peach-tinged skin. Zach felt a ridiculous sense of elation that it hadn't been her body on the screen. He didn't want anyone else feasting on those lush curves, those fine, full breasts.

Rebecca started to move closer to him, but he held her off.

"I smell like charred wood. I should…shower."

She leaned her head against his shoulder. "I like the smell." Her lips pressed to his ear, a huge ache filling her. "I can't wait, Zach." She let out a small, low moan to punctuate her need.

Her whispered words were like a fierce white heat shooting through him and he ripped at his clothes, Rebecca helping him. The two of them naked, they wrapped their arms around each other, body to body, a perfect fit.

He took her right there in the kitchen, hoisting her up against the counter, both of them too far gone for preambles or foreplay. She raised her hips, straddled him, their bodies speaking in a language that burned and consumed, driven on by an almost-unbearable urgency. He entered her in one hard, fluid thrust, which she welcomed with a wild cry of pleasure. He felt like a fireman answering an alarm—one that was ringing inside his head as well as hers, and wouldn't quit.

As their bodies connected with ferocity, so did their mouths—hard, feverish kisses, tongues sparring, breaths coming in shallow gasps. Rebecca clung to him. She had never felt so wild, so free of inhibition, so utterly consumed by passion. Wave after wave of release shook through her body until she cried out in wanton pleasure. Within moments, Zach was joining her, his cries mingling with hers.

When they broke apart, neither of them knew what to say, both of them dreading the awkward silence. Then they smelled something odd—something burning. A moment of sheer panic engulfed them until they discovered the source, breaking out into a gale of laughter when they saw that the pan on the lit stove was sizzling, the water having boiled away.

ZACH SHOWERED AND dressed hurriedly. When he walked into the living room, Rebecca was sprawled on his sofa, fast asleep. She was dressed in a clean pair of jeans, a gray sweatshirt, and she'd put her hair up in a ponytail. It was hard to reconcile this demure young woman with the wanton temptress he'd tangled with in the kitchen less than an hour earlier.

He got a blanket from his bedroom and covered her gently with it. Her eyes flickered open. "Zach?"

He stroked her cheek lightly. "It's okay. Go back to sleep."

"I'll just…take a little…nap…and then we'll…get going."

"Right," he murmured, tucking her in, then slipping quietly out the door.

REBECCA WAS AWAKENED by the shrill ring of the phone. Groggily, her eyes still closed, she reached out her hand for the receiver. It wasn't there. Someone had moved the phone. Her maid? Gail? She rolled over, only to land with a startled thud on the floor. Her eyes popped open. It took a few seconds for it to penetrate that she wasn't in her lush Malibu bedroom; another few seconds to realize exactly where she was.

The phone stopped ringing. Now she heard a familiar surly voice: "I'm out. Leave a message. I'll get back to you."

Rebecca struggled to her feet. Out? Out where? How could Zach have gone off without her after everything that had happened?

Pushing aside her irritation, Rebecca held her breath as she waited to hear who was on the other end of the line. The torch telling Zach of yet another fire? Eileen with a change of heart? Rebecca's own heart started beating erratically.

She stared at the phone, completely taken aback when she heard another familiar voice come on the line.

"Mr. Chapin, this is Sam Porter, Rebecca Fox's agent...."

Rebecca dived for the phone. "Sam?"

"Rebecca?"

"What's up, Sam? Why are you calling Zach?"

"I wasn't calling Zach. I was trying to track you down. Have you gone nuts, Rebecca? Have you completely lost it?"

Rebecca smiled. "Not completely, Sam."

"This is no time for jokes. Look, enough is enough. Now, I've already spoken to Gail. She's got a first-class ticket waiting for you at Logan airport. The flight takes off at five this afternoon. I'll pick you up myself at LAX...."

"Slow down, Sam. I'm not going anywhere. At least not for another three weeks. What are you so worked up about, anyway?"

"What am I so worked up about? What am I—? Have you seen the morning papers? Have you listened to the news on TV, radio?"

"No. No, I just woke up." She looked down at her watch, astonished to realize it was almost two in the afternoon.

There was a long pause on Sam's end. "I see."

"I fell asleep on the couch, Sam. Zach isn't even here." She didn't want her agent getting the wrong idea, even if it was the right idea.

"Okay, okay, it's none of my business. But risking your beautiful neck by rescuing two runaways trapped in a burning building, that is my business."

"But how...?"

"How? How? You're a celebrity, Rebecca. And now you're a hero. You and this irresponsible idiot, Chapin—"

"He's not an irresponsible idiot, Sam. He's...an incredible, complex, deeply committed man."

"That's not what you told Gail yesterday evening."

Rebecca smiled. "Well, I...got to know him better. And besides," she quickly went on, "he was even angrier than you are at my having played superhero. He'd ordered me to wait outside."

"Rebecca, Rebecca..."

"I know, Sam. It doesn't make a lot of sense to me, either."

"Take the five o'clock, honey."

"I can't. Besides, as my agent, you should be crowing. Think what effect this will have on Mason. I wouldn't be surprised if he comes begging to you to let me play Toni Paradisi now."

"If he does, will you come home?"

Rebecca hesitated. That was the whole point of all this, wasn't it? Or was it? Things had definitely taken on a decidedly new slant.

"Look, as your agent I'll crow," Sam said. "As someone who cares about you, I'll be worried sick until you come back," he added gently.

"I'll stay out of burning buildings from now on. How's that? So you don't have to worry, okay?"

"I have the feeling that's not all there is to worry about."

Rebecca had to smile. Her agent knew her very well, indeed. "I know this...relationship isn't too likely to go anywhere, Sam. I'm sure Zach would tell you that in spades. Maybe it'll be just one of those...brief but magical interludes. Two people who happened to be together at the right time, the right place..."

Sam's sigh hummed over the line. "That's a great closing speech from a movie script, Rebecca. But in real life, things don't always work out so tidily."

WHEN ZACH WALKED INTO the fire commissioner's office, he found Fitzgerald pacing. Always a bad sign.

"Where the hell were you? I told Collins to have you here two hours ago," Fitzgerald barked.

"I was at the hospital," Zach said evenly. "Keeping a scared kid company while his brother was in surgery having skin grafts."

Fitzgerald slammed a fist down on the morning edition of one of the Boston dailies. Rebecca Fox's picture was splashed across the front page right next to a shot of a burning building. "I suppose you saw this already."

Zach nodded. "Someone in the crowd or from the press must have recognized her."

"I gave you strict orders, Chapin...."

"Yeah, well, I told you from the get-go that I was the wrong guy for the baby-sitting job," Zach retorted.

"Not only did you ignore my orders to keep Miss Fox out of danger, you have continued to be involved in a case that I personally had you pulled from."

Zach placed both palms on Fitzgerald's desk. "This creep is mine."

"That's where you're wrong, Chapin. Collins was right. You've let yourself get too personally involved in this case. You've lost your perspective. Your judgment. Once that happens, you start to get careless. You begin taking unnecessary risks. You get yourself in real hot water. Do you know what I'm saying?"

Zach nodded. He had to agree with Fitzgerald. Only he wasn't thinking about his personal involvement in the arson case. He was thinking about his personal involvement with Hollywood movie star cum recent local heroine, Rebecca Fox.

Fitzgerald gave him a level look. "Get yourself under control, Chapin."

"You're right," Zach said. "That's just what I have to do."

REBECCA RAN INTO JOE Kelly in the hallway outside the bureau. He smiled at her. "You look better. Not that you ever look bad, mind you...."

She looked past him to the office door. "Is he in?"

Joe shook his head.

Rebecca wasn't sure she believed him. She started for the door. Joe caught hold of her arm. "I wouldn't go in there unless you want to be greeted by a rowdy round of applause from the other guys on the squad. It's not every day that a movie queen plays fire fighter/rescuer."

"Where is he, Joe? I went down to the hospital. He'd been and gone. The social worker there told me he stuck around until he was sure Jerry made it through surgery okay and then he took his brother, Tod, over to a church shelter. I stopped at the shelter, but I missed him again. I'm beginning to get the feeling he's avoiding me. You know him pretty well, Joe. What feeling are you getting?"

Joe grinned, spinning her around to face the stairs—and Zach, who had just wearily finished climbing up them. "Always go directly to the source whenever possible," Joe whispered, giving her a little nudge in Zach's direction.

Rebecca was about to give Zach a piece of her mind for taking off on her that morning, but he looked so haggard, so beat, so gritty, and so damn sexy, she didn't have the heart. A heart that was already doing flip-flops.

"You look like you could use a good meal and then bed," she said firmly.

Joe sauntered by. "Should I still tell Millie to expect you over tonight?" he asked Rebecca glibly.

"Yes," Zach said firmly even before Rebecca had the chance to open her mouth to answer.

Joe chuckled as he headed down the stairs.

"You didn't have to worry, Zach," Rebecca said, trying to keep the hurt out of her voice. "I haven't changed my plans. Any of them."

He strode past her. "Well, I have."

She hurried after him. "What does that mean?"

He stopped abruptly and spun around. "Don't you see what's happening here? This whole thing isn't working out. Thanks to your derring-do last night, I've got Collins and Fitzgerald breathing down my neck to protect your neck at all costs and stay off this case or I'll have my walking papers. And talking about walking, when I walked out of my building this morning I was accosted by a hungry pack of reporters looking for the inside scoop on movie-star-turned-undercover-arson-investigator, Rebecca Fox. The only reason you got any sleep was I told them you were staying at the Heritage."

"What about you? Did you get any sleep?"

Zach shrugged off her question.

"No wonder you're in such a foul mood."

He threw up his hands. "Don't you get it? You've turned my whole world upside down. My head hasn't stopped spinning...."

Rebecca smiled playfully. "Neither has mine."

"No, that's not what I'm talking about," he snapped. Only he knew that, at this point, he was incapable of separating their professional partnership from the very personal one that was developing between them at rapid-fire speed.

"Don't you think we should talk about it, Zach?"

"No." He stuck a cigarette in his mouth.

Rebecca plucked it out before he got it lit. "Let me buy you dinner. Something that comes on a real plate. In a place with real linen napkins and cloth tablecloths."

"Surrounded by a pack of real paparazzi?" he said grumpily.

"My personal manager issued a story to the media. By tonight, somebody else will be news. What do you say? We could both use a decent meal."

"All right," he conceded. "But I don't want to talk about anything," he added pointedly. "I'm too beat. Do you understand?"

Rebecca raised her right hand in a pledge. "Absolutely. We won't talk about anything."

"DID YOU LOVE HER?"

Zach looked up sharply from his plate of trout almondine. Rebecca suppressed a smile. They were sitting across from each other in a quiet corner of a casually elegant seafood restaurant on Lewis Wharf.

"Eileen?" he asked edgily. The truth was he hadn't given Eileen so much as a passing thought since that Dear John phone message she'd left for him. Too many other thoughts had been clouding his mind. And they all began with *Rebecca*.

"No, not Eileen. Cheryl."

Zach put down his fork. "Cheryl?"

"Your wife. Your ex-wife," Rebecca corrected.

"I know who Cheryl is," he said irritably. "We were married for five years. And divorced for three. I suppose you know that."

"Facts don't give the whole picture, Zach."

He took a sip of his wine, then forced a cavalier expression. "Sure, I loved her. I married her, didn't I?"

Rebecca carefully buttered a crusty piece of French bread. "What was she like? What made you fall in love with her?"

He felt supremely uncomfortable. Having feelings was one thing for Zach. Talking about them, analyzing them, was another thing altogether. "I don't know. We were young, we dated for a couple of years, she thought it was about time.... Her family thought so, too."

"You didn't want to get married?" Rebecca pressed.

Zach sighed. "Sure, I did." He took a bite of trout, chewed, set down his fork. "Okay, maybe I was ambivalent. You hear tales."

"Tales?" Rebecca asked.

"From other firemen. It's tough on wives. The hours, the tensions, the danger. Cheryl tried to convince me she could hack it." He grew silent.

"She couldn't?" Rebecca asked softly.

"That's pretty obvious. She left me, didn't she?"

"That must have been pretty tough on you."

Zach's expression hardened. Not a man who took well to sympathy. "Don't go thinking our marriage was a bed of roses. We fought plenty. We didn't see eye-to-eye on a lot of things. I look back on it now and I see it was probably a mistake from the beginning."

"Why?" she persisted.

Zach didn't answer right away. "Why? Because there's loving and there's loving. Maybe we just never really loved each other enough to make it through the hard times. Our marriage just sort of unwound, like one of those windup toys."

They ate in silence for a few minutes. Then Zach looked over at her.

"Tell me something. How come you're asking me about Cheryl, who I haven't been involved with for years, instead of Eileen, who only just dumped me?"

She grinned. "Maybe I'm going in chronological order."

Zach wasn't amused. He turned away, pretending to be checking for hidden reporters around the restaurant.

"I didn't ask about Eileen because I think I know the answer," Rebecca said seriously.

He returned his gaze to her. "And what's the answer?"

"You didn't love her. And that's the way you wanted it. A nice, casual affair. No demands, no obligations, no responsibilities, no broken hearts."

He smiled ruefully. "You've been watching too many Hollywood movies. Or, I guess I should say, acting in them."

"I bet there hasn't been anyone since Cheryl. I think you've been real scared of getting burned again."

"In my business, you're smart to be scared of getting burned."

"I'm talking about your off-hours, Zach. I'm talking about what happened between us—"

"I thought we weren't going to talk about this stuff." He took another, longer swallow of wine.

"By 'this stuff' I take it you mean what we're each feeling about the wild, passionate lovemaking we engaged in this morning in your kitchen?" she inquired insouciantly.

Zach's face reddened and he coughed on the wine he'd just swallowed. "Why don't you just announce it on the loudspeaker?"

She leaned closer and slipped her hand over his. "I'd

never had sex in the kitchen before. I wouldn't mind trying the rest of the rooms in your apartment, Zach."

He pulled his hand away. "Quit it. What happened this morning was a...fluke. We were both...flying high because we'd rescued those kids. Our adrenaline was flowing. We were overtired, strung tight—"

"Was it as good for you as it was for me, Zach? Because it was a red-letter experience for me." Her eyes sparkled. "I never felt so...fired up."

He shut his eyes. "Why are you doing this to me? Just because you're a movie star..."

"Was that who you were making love to in your kitchen this morning? A movie star? Or was it me?"

"You can't separate the two," he argued.

"You can if you want to. Acting is just something I do for a living."

"You don't take acting any more casually than I take investigating arson."

"Okay," she conceded. "That's true. But neither acting or arson investigating had anything to do with what happened between us in your kitchen."

He rolled his eyes, agitation and arousal having an all-out war inside him. "You know what my mistake was? I should have carried you off to the bedroom. If it had been more conventional..."

She laughed. "You're not a conventional person. Neither am I."

"That's what worries me."

"Maybe that's not all that worries you. To set the record straight, Zach, I never had any intention of letting something like this happen. It was the last thing in the world— Let's face it, you're not exactly choice material for a relationship. You're a very difficult person. Stubborn, rude, irritable..."

"You're right. You ought to stick to your leading men. Like the one in that movie..."

"You've been reading too many tabloids. I'm not one

of those actresses who falls for all her leading men and jumps in the sack with them first chance she gets. I avoid actors like the plague. Any man in the business, for that matter. It gets to be just too Hollywood. The last man I was involved with was a real-estate broker. That was close to a year ago. He was very nice, very sensitive, and, unfortunately, very...dull. You, on the other hand, are anything but dull."

He poured himself another glass of wine, avoiding eye contact. "Look, why don't you eat your...your shrimp? They're getting cold."

"What are we going to do, Zach? Spend the next three weeks together trying to deny that we have this incredible physical attraction for each other?"

"Are you always this blunt?"

She leaned forward. "You think I was scared when we were in that burning building? It's nothing to how scared I am right now. I'm no better at this sort of thing than you are," she said quietly.

Zach stared at her. Rebecca Fox was like no other woman he'd ever met. Wily and provocative one minute, earnest and vulnerable the next. He was scared, too. Only he'd never been a man to expose those kinds of feelings.

He didn't answer right away. "It isn't going to work. Go home, Rebecca."

"What about our torch?"

"*Our* torch?" He pushed aside his plate. "Oh, no..."

"You can't shut me out, Zach. Something happened to me in that fire. I can't explain it exactly, but when I think of those two kids...of that poor homeless man who died in that other fire... When I think of all the other possible victims... Oh, Zach, let me help you."

"You'll get me fired."

"Is that really what you're afraid of?" For all the fire commissioner's threats, Rebecca seriously doubted he'd hand one of Boston's top arson investigators his walking papers, especially after Zach brought the arsonist in on a silver platter. She seriously doubted Zach thought so, either.

Zach didn't answer.

She folded her hands on the table, donned a demure expression. "What if I promise to stay out of burning buildings from now on?" She gave a flicker of a smile. "And out of your kitchen?"

ZACH WAS DRIVING Rebecca to Joe Kelly's house in Somerville. He was in a foul mood, blaming it on lack of sleep and too much wine at dinner. "You know what the real problem is, here?"

"Tell me," she said calmly.

"We live in two different worlds. I live in a world of harsh reality. You live in a fantasy world. Our whole orientation to life is different. The whole way we see things is different."

"I wasn't born an actress, Zach. What if I told you I was raised on the mean streets of Detroit? What if I told you my dad was a postal clerk and my mom ran out on us when I was eleven? What if I told you I had to work in a grocery store after school just to help make ends meet? What if I told you my older brother was in a gang and was in and out of reform schools and ended up doing three to five in the state pen for armed robbery?"

He shot her a dubious look. "I'd ask you what movie it was from."

She grinned. "*Cry for Help*. The second film I made. My first starring role. Unfortunately, the studio went belly-up and the movie got shelved. Not that I was too broken up about it. The story was pretty clichéd," she added with a smile.

"You're too much."

"Want the real scoop?"

"No." He didn't want to get to know her any better. He already knew more than he could cope with.

She ignored him. "I was born in Santa Monica, a real California girl. My dad was a producer, but he's in finance now. My mom was a promising soprano, sang in light opera for a while, but after I came along she devoted herself to being a happy homemaker. I was spoiled rotten, always got everything I wanted, and what I wanted most was to be an actress. Oh, sure, I had a couple of years where I struggled, but I never had to resort to working in a grocery store to make ends meet. My ends have always met."

He smiled crookedly. "And you thought the movie was clichéd?"

She laughed.

Zach couldn't stop himself from thinking she had an incredibly sexy laugh. That thought led to another. She could be laughing like that next to him in his bed instead of his car. So why was he driving her to Somerville? For a minute he was tempted to make a wild U-turn. What the hell was wrong with partaking in some fantasy for a change?

"So what's your life story, Zach?"

Rebecca's question brought him sharply back to harsh reality.

"My life story?" His tone was curt and cynical. "I was raised on the mean streets of South Boston. My dad wasn't a postal clerk. He was a drunk. My mom didn't walk out on us—us being me and my two brothers and three sisters—she held down two jobs so that we wouldn't get thrown out of our cockroach-ridden three-bedroom walk-up. I didn't work in a grocery store, but I did practically everything else to make a buck. I never wound up in reform school, but I might have. Luckily, I had an uncle who was a fireman. He took me out with him a few times, got me hooked. I became a fireman, but after a few years I realized I wanted to do more than fight fires. I wanted to fight the bastards who were starting some of them. The rest, as they say, is history."

Rebecca stared at Zach's hardened profile as he kept his eyes straight ahead on the road. "And now you've got me hooked," she said quietly.

They both knew she was talking about more than hunting down arsonists.

THE KELLY FAMILY LIVED in a small but tidy white-shingled two-story house that was trimmed with green shutters. Boston Celtics green. There was a basketball hoop over the attached single-car garage. It looked like it got a lot of use.

It was close to nine o'clock when Zach pulled into the driveway, but all the lights in the Kelly house were on. A white cotton café curtain in one of the downstairs rooms facing the driveway was pulled back, a young girl's face peeking out for a moment. Zach waved, then turned to Rebecca.

"Appears the whole Rebecca Fox fan club is waiting up for you."

Rebecca gave him a plaintive look. "Come in with me."

"I'm beat." He was wearing that "closed-up shop" expression on his face.

"Please, Zach. Just for a couple of minutes." For all her celebrity status, Rebecca had never quite made peace with being one. Being an actress was what it was about, not being a "star." The adulation never sat easily with her, even though she could take advantage of it when she had to, as she'd done with Boston's fire commissioner.

Zach tapped his fingers on the steering wheel, debating with himself, all the while knowing he'd acquiesce. He was starting to worry whether there was anything he was going to be able to deny the irrepressible Rebecca Fox.

7

JOE KELLY OPENED THE Christmas-wreath-decorated front door as Zach and Rebecca started up the path. Rebecca emitted a little gasp of alarm as she saw at least a dozen excited figures gathered behind Joe.

"Who are all those people?" she whispered anxiously to Zach. "I thought it was just Joe, his wife and their two kids."

Joe was edged out of the doorway by a large woman whose dark hair was generously sprinkled with gray. She was decked out in a bright blue print dress, large blue button earrings and matching blue pumps. Her hands were pressed together in delight as Rebecca, nudged along by Zach, started up the front steps.

"I'm Millie Kelly," the woman in blue said eagerly. "Come in. Come in. We've all been waiting. I hope you don't mind that a few neighbors came over. And of course there was no keeping Joe's mother away, or my two brothers and their families. How often does a famous movie star come to Somerville? When Mr. Fitzgerald called and asked me if we would mind putting you up... Mind? I was ecstatic."

Millie slipped an arm through Rebecca's as she spoke in animated rapid-fire fashion, guiding her into the narrow hallway crowded with eager friends and relatives of the Kellys. To her chagrin, Rebecca saw now that she'd underestimated the number of "fans" by at least half.

Millie paused, but only to address her husband.

"Why, Joe, you're absolutely right," she exclaimed. "She's even more beautiful in person."

Joe winked at Zach who was hanging back, tempted to make a fast getaway—until he caught Rebecca's plaintive look. He sidled inside the house.

There was a hushed silence and rapt attention from everyone in the hallway as Rebecca took off her parka and flashed the gathering a smile. Millie made the introductions—to a sea of names and faces, few of whom Rebecca was likely to remember, but she acted as if each one would be indelibly printed on her mind. Millie's lanky and awkward sixteen-year-old son, Joe Junior, gave her a smitten look as she signed an autograph for him. Abbie, the Kellys' fourteen-year-old daughter, who shielded her mouth with her hand to hide her new braces, confided in Rebecca that she, too, wanted to be an actress.

Joe's mother, Rose, a petite, sprightly gray-haired woman, quickly took charge of the "event," guiding Rebecca into the small dining room, the lace-covered table overflowing with fruits, cakes, candies and a goodly assortment of liquor bottles. Everyone followed, the whole group wedged together around the generous spread. Zach's eyes strayed from the bottle of Scotch on one corner of the table to the movie poster of Rebecca hanging up on the back wall. The same poster that had seduced him into entering that video store the night before. A sudden rush of arousal blanketed him, paralyzing him for a moment. He couldn't unglue his eyes from the poster. He couldn't unglue his mind from the memory of those lusty antics he and Rebecca had engaged in in the kitchen. It had almost been as if they were making love and waging war at the same time. He started drifting into a red-hot reverie.

Joe followed Zach's frozen gaze. "Courtesy of Millie's brother, Gus. He's working over at Video Vista now. Nice touch, huh? One of these days I'm gonna have to get around to renting the video. Maybe you can come over, I'll microwave some popcorn and we'll watch it together."

Zach scowled, forcefully pulling his eyes away from the poster, careful not to let them fall on Rebecca in the flesh. "I've gotta get back home. I haven't slept in twenty-four hours," he croaked hoarsely.

Unfortunately for Zach, Millie overheard him. "You haven't slept in twenty-four hours and you're going to drive back to the city? You could fall asleep at the wheel. Why, that's just what happened to my brother, Buddy, last year. Buddy," she called out, but he didn't hear her over the din, everyone jockeying for position and vying for a few words with the celebrated movie star.

"I won't fall asleep at the wheel. I promise," Zach said.

Millie was not a woman to be argued with. "You'll sleep over. Joe Junior's got bunk beds. I'll clear this crowd out before ten and you and Miss Fox will have some peace and quiet. After what you've both been through, I'm sure you need it."

Zach and Joe shared a look as Millie bustled off to see to her famous houseguest, shouting, "Stop crowding her. Give her a chance to breathe. Joe Junior, cut Miss Fox a piece of that chocolate chiffon cake."

"Ma, will you please stop with the 'Junior,'" Joe Junior muttered. "It makes me sound like I'm a kid."

As she was plied with everything from Millie's chocolate chiffon cake to Rose Kelly's homemade peach liqueur, Rebecca tried to graciously answer questions and accept showers of compliments.

"I've seen all of your movies, Miss Fox. Of course, it's only my opinion, but as far as I'm concerned you put Julia Roberts to shame. Why, your last picture…"

"Did you really help rescue those boys in that burning building last night? Or was it part of a publicity stunt? It's so hard to believe everything you read in the papers...."

"Honestly, who is your favorite leading man? It must be almost impossible not to fall in love with each and every one of them. Or, do you...?"

"Isn't it hard doing those love scenes? I just can't imagine...."

"Will you be filming your new movie here in Boston? I would give anything to play an extra. I've actually had some acting experience...."

"It must be so exciting dining in all those fancy restaurants, going to parties with all those famous people...."

Zach stayed out of the fray, trying to figure out how to make a clean getaway. If he spent another night under the same roof as Rebecca, he was sure he wouldn't get any sleep. And he was almost punch-drunk with exhaustion at this point.

Joe brought him over a glass of Scotch. "Here. You look like you could use it."

Zach smiled crookedly. "I could, which is why I'd better abstain."

Joe eyed him contemplatively.

Discomforted by his partner's close examination, Zach shifted away from the topic. "Anything come back from the labs yet?"

"No," Joe said. "But they promised me there'd be a report on my desk first thing tomorrow morning. How about the little kid? Todd, right? He see anything?"

Zach shrugged. "Says not, but he was so worried about his brother and still so shaken up himself, I don't know if we have the whole story yet. I'll drop down to the shelter tomorrow and have another chat with him."

"And his brother? When do you think we'll be able to get a statement from him?"

"A couple of days, anyway. I'll have to leave him to you and Adams. If Collins gets wind that I've gone back down to the hospital, he'll start raking me over the coals again."

"Or worse still, send you back down to the principal's office," Joe quipped.

"Yeah, right." Zach hesitated. "What'd you do about that button Rebecca found?"

"First I took it around to a few men's shops," Joe said. "Consensus was, it came off one of those budget-priced raincoats you can buy in most department stores. Found one over at Filenes Basement store that had the exact same buttons. Thirty-nine ninety-five. I bought it. Might even be your size," Joe added with a grin.

"Dandy."

"I put in a call to the manufacturer. Described the coat, the buttons. It's a discontinued style. They'd stopped making it a couple of years ago. I guess that's how come the one I tracked down ended up in a bargain-basement store."

Zach's eyes strayed to Rebecca who seemed to be basking in all the attention. "It could be the button was from the torch's coat, I suppose. Not that it means much."

Joe followed Zach's gaze. "She's quite a hit with everyone. They can't get enough of her." He paused for a few beats. "A lot of guys would love to be in your shoes, my friend."

Zach's eyes dropped to his worn cordovan loafers. "They just think they would." He gave Joe's shoulder a squeeze. "I've really got to get out of here."

Joe smiled. "Okay, I'll tackle Millie if she tries to stop you. Just don't go nodding off behind the wheel and cracking up or she'll never let me hear the end of it."

Zach slipped out of the house and was about to get in his car when he caught sight of the curtain in the living room being pulled back.

On the pretense of having to use the powder room,

Rebecca had slipped into the living room, which faced onto the driveway. She looked out the frost-tinged window at Zach. Their eyes met and held for a few moments. "See you tomorrow morning," she mouthed. He gave a half nod as he slipped in behind the wheel and drove off.

Rebecca's hand fell away from the curtain at the sound of a voice behind her.

"He's a stubborn man."

Rebecca turned to face Joe's wife. "Yes, he is."

"You like him, don't you?" Millie coaxed.

It was a very charged question—one that Rebecca wasn't capable of answering cavalierly. "I don't really know him. We only...just met." She stared down at the brown carpeted floor.

"I've known Zach for years, and I still don't really know him either, but I'm crazy about him," Millie said with a grin. "So is Joe. So are the kids. They're plenty taken with you, too. And it isn't only because you're famous. You're a nice person—not at all what you imagine a movie star might be. You don't put on airs. Which is a good thing, because we're just plain folk. And we all want you to feel right at home here."

Rebecca smiled, fighting back a yawn. "You've already made me feel that way."

"You're exhausted. I'll shoo everyone out and have Abbie show you to your room. It's not the Ritz or anything, but it's clean and I've warned the kids not to go blasting their music when they wake up for school."

"Oh, I don't mind. I have to be up early anyway so I can drive into the bureau with Joe. I don't want Zach riding me for showing up late for duty." As if he would. Rebecca knew his fondest hope was that she wouldn't show up at all. Somehow, she had to convince her partner that she could be a real help to him.

Millie put a hand on Rebecca's shoulder. "You be

careful. Dealing with arsonists is a dangerous business, as you found out last night."

Rebecca nodded, thinking to herself that the same was true of dealing with arson investigators.

ONLY THE MAN'S BREATH was visible in the cold night air as he once again hid in the shadows. He observed the burned-out building with disgust, tapping the rolled-up newspaper in his hand. Once again, Zachary Chapin was splashed across the front pages—a hero. Even his big-time, movie-star girlfriend had gotten in on the act. Now, if they'd been two *dead* heroes, that would have been one thing. Two for the price of one. He smiled. He liked that.

A gust of wind sent a chill through him. He pulled up the collar of his raincoat and went to close the top button only to find it was missing. For about a minute, he thought about where it might have fallen off, but then forgot about the button when he saw the familiar battered red Ford pull into a parking space on the other side of the street.

He stepped deeper into the shadows, watching Chapin get out of his car. He wondered where the movie-star girlfriend was. That was one beauty he was sure the arson investigator wouldn't let slip easily through his hands.

Pure hatred enveloped him as he watched Chapin head for his building. He noticed the slight limp, took some consolation in the "hero's" imperfection. Most of all, he consoled himself with the knowledge that everything had its time and its place.

Two for the price of one. Yes, he liked that. An extra bonus. And then there was that kid. Definitely a loose end that needed tying up.

He stepped out of the shadows and headed down the street for the "T" stop where he'd catch the green line into Dorchester and Father Frank Malrooney's shelter.

As soon as Zach stepped into his apartment he could detect the lingering hint of Rebecca's exotic perfume. When he flicked on the light in his living room, he saw the blanket he'd covered her with that morning, neatly folded on the couch where she'd slept. His stomach growled. He hadn't eaten much of his fancy dinner and he was hungry, but he couldn't get himself to walk into his kitchen. Afraid being in there would resurrect too many memories.

Hell, who was he kidding? The memories were already deeply embedded in him, the feelings still reverberating through his whole body—that all-consuming desire, that burning intensity, the obsessive need to possess her, to be possessed. Never before, not even when it was new and fresh and exciting with Cheryl, never before had it been like it had been with Rebecca.

He strode into the kitchen like a man resolved to confront his demons and conquer them. The minute he walked in there, though, he felt his throat tighten up, his heart shift into overdrive. His gaze fell on the counter where he'd taken her, and suddenly he was reliving those sizzling minutes. He could vividly picture her robe falling away, his eyes feasting on that exquisite statuesque body that looked too perfect to be real. Then he was kissing her, tearing at his clothes, lifting her off her feet, pressing her up against the counter. Her legs were encircling him, her voice beseeching him....

The jangle of the telephone jarred him from his reminiscence. He wiped a bead of sweat from his brow as he went to answer it, grateful for the interruption. Reminiscences like that would only lead to trouble. As if he wasn't already up to his neck in trouble. With a capital T.

"Yeah?"

There was silence on the other end of the line. Zach's feeling of relief was short-lived. His whole body went on instant alert.

"Get to the point, or it's adios," he said sharply, in no mood for games.

No response. He was about to hang up.

"Mr. Chapin?"

Zach gripped the receiver tighter. The voice was hesitant, high-pitched, young. He closed his eyes for a moment. "Todd? Is that you?"

"Yes."

Zach checked his watch. It was close to ten. "Shouldn't you be in bed, Todd? Father Frank runs a tight ship over at the shelter. You don't want to make a bad first impression by breaking the rules."

"No… It's just… I couldn't sleep."

"Yeah, I know how it is," Zach said softly, because he did. How many nights had he been too haunted, too frightened, too worried to sleep?

"You really think Jerry's gonna be okay, Mr. Chapin?"

"As good as new." Zach packed an extra dose of assurance into his voice.

"I guess it was pretty dumb hiding out in that closed-up building. Only we were so cold, Mr. Chapin. And we had nowhere to go."

"What about your folks?"

"They split up last year. Neither of them wanted us. We stayed with an aunt for a while, but she didn't seem to like us much. Always complained that we ate too much, took up too much room, cost her too much money. Then there was her…boyfriend…." Todd's voice trailed off.

Zach gritted his teeth. He'd seen the old bruises on the boy's arms. "You won't have to go back there, Todd. Father Frank will do everything he can to find you a decent home. You and Jerry. Don't worry about it now. Trust me. Everything's gonna work out fine."

"Mr. Chapin?"

"Yeah?"

"You said someone started that fire on purpose."

Zach leaned against the wall. "That's right, Todd. And I'm going to find him and make him pay. You have my word on that."

"Mr. Chapin, I think maybe I did see someone."

Zach sprang off the wall, but he kept his tone very even. "Tell me about it, Todd."

"It wasn't inside the building. That's what you were asking me before. I did see this guy outside, though. Just before I started to smell smoke. He was on the street, looking up at the building."

The muscles in Zach's stomach constricted. "Did he see you, Todd?"

"I don't know. I'm not sure."

"Can you describe him for me, Todd?"

"Not really. It was dark. I just saw this guy in a dark raincoat."

A dark raincoat. With a missing button, most likely, Zach thought. "How old did he look, Todd? Could you tell what color his hair was?"

"No. No, I gotta go, Mr. Chapin. I just heard footsteps. I don't wanna get caught breaking the rules. This place is okay."

"Don't worry about the rules, Todd. I'll clear you with Father Frank—" Before he finished he heard the phone click, the line going dead.

Zach quickly dialed his friend, Police Lieutenant Lou Denehy at the Forty-Second Precinct over in Dorchester and arranged for round-the-clock surveillance of the shelter, and especially of Todd.

After he hung up, he trudged out of the kitchen, no longer the least bit hungry. He stepped into the living room, glanced over at his bedroom door, but in the end he stretched out on his couch, covering himself with the same blanket he'd used to cover Rebecca the night before. Her scent clung to the wool. He pressed the material to his face, breathing in deeply. It was nuts, he knew. But it helped him fall asleep.

REBECCA COULDN'T SLEEP. It had nothing to do with being in a narrow bed in an unfamiliar room thousands of miles away from her luxurious oceanfront Malibu digs. She couldn't sleep because she felt unglued, as if a hurricane had swept right through her. Hurricane Zach Chapin. Lying in her bed in the Kellys' spare room, she tried to assess the damage in the aftermath of the storm. Physically, she was still in one piece, although there'd been a few terrified minutes back in that raging inferno of a building when she hadn't been sure she'd make it out alive, never mind in one piece. Emotionally... That was another story altogether. Her mind was fragmented, her feelings in a whirlpool. She tried to tell herself that what she was feeling for the irascible Zach Chapin was purely sexual—a temporary sexual obsession. Ever since that passionate explosion in his kitchen, she'd been tormented by desire for him. When she'd woken up on his couch that afternoon, her real disappointment hadn't been that he'd gone off to work without her. It was that he wasn't there, sweeping her up into his arms, making love to her again. She really had wanted them to try out every room in his apartment—sex in the shower, on the beige carpet covering his living-room floor, on his dinette table, even going for convention and doing it in his bed. When she'd offered to take him out to dinner that evening, where she really wanted to take him was to the nearest motel. When he was driving her to the Kellys' place, she had to fight back the urge to grab hold of the wheel and insist he turn the car around and take her back to his apartment.

She sat up in bed, tossing off the blanket. She'd gone and worked herself up into quite a sweat. She pushed a damp strand of auburn hair from her face, angry at herself for getting so carried away. She needed these feelings like a hole in her head. A relationship with Zach was utterly untenable. He'd been right, even if it was a tired cliché. They lived in two different worlds. In three weeks she'd be back in Hollywood, back in gear, back on her own home turf, and this would all seem like some strange, haunting film—someone else's film that she had accidentally stepped into.

Only this was no film, no fantasy. This was, as Zach had so succinctly put it, harsh reality. Two boys had nearly died in a fire started by an arsonist last night. She and Zach could as easily have been victims, as well. She shivered as she remembered that horrible charred corpse in the morgue—a man who hadn't been as lucky as they. Pulling the covers back up over her shoulders, she closed her eyes, hearing in her mind the voice of the torch on Zach's phone. A twisted voice filled with venom. A voice that basked in a warped kind of power and control. A voice without compassion.

Why did he always call Zach? Was it, as Zach insisted, simply that the torch singled him out because he had received the most 'notoriety' in the media for bringing in arsonists? Did this warped man merely want to one-up the star investigator? Or was there something more personal in this? Could the torch have a special vendetta against Zach?

Too restless and on edge to sleep, Rebecca finally got out of bed and quietly slipped downstairs to make herself a cup of warm milk. The house was still and dark. Imagining everyone had gone to bed, she was surprised to see a light on in the kitchen.

Joe Kelly was sitting at the knotty-pine kitchen table, reading the newspaper and finishing off the last of his wife's chocolate chiffon cake with a large glass of milk. He looked up nervously when she walked in, but then smiled with relief.

"Phew. I thought it was Millie. She'd give me hell for

this." He pointed to his late-night snack. "I've got high cholesterol. And—" he patted his paunch "—the doc wants me to lose a few pounds."

"I won't snitch on you, but your diet's as bad as Zach's," Rebecca scolded him lightly. "Before I leave I ought to sit you both down and give you a few lessons in proper nutrition."

Joe took a bite of cake. "So, when are you leaving?" he asked in a failed attempt at sounding casual.

Rebecca folded her arms across her chest. "You, too?"

"Don't get me wrong, Rebecca. I'm real impressed by what you did last night. Not a lot of civilians would have been as brave, as gutsy...."

"As crazy?"

He grinned. "That, too."

"So why are you so eager to see me leave?"

Joe hesitated. "It's just that I hate seeing my old buddy put through the wringer," he said softly. "He hasn't had it very easy."

"I know." Forgetting about her warm milk, she sat down across from Joe.

"No, you don't. You may know some of the facts, but you don't know the half of it. Zach could win an Academy Award for making it look like he's got it all under control. Funny part is, he's actually got it more under control than he realizes."

Joe tapped his temple. "Inside, the guy feels like he's hanging by a thread. You walk into his life and suddenly he starts worrying that the thread's gonna fray and break."

"I don't want to hurt him, Joe. I don't want to put him through the wringer."

Joe looked at her head-on. "What do you want from him, Rebecca? You're a movie star. You hobnob with the rich and famous. Hell, you *are* the rich and famous.

Zach's a regular guy. He's about as unglamorous as they make 'em."

Rebecca could feel her face heat up. She took a swallow of Joe's milk. "You make it sound like what's happening makes some sense. To either of us. I doubt Zach could sort it out any better than I can."

"My guess is, he'll still be trying long after you're back in Tinseltown."

"My guess is, so will I."

Joe started to take another piece of cake, but ended up pushing aside the plate. "You mean that, don't you?"

"I've never felt like this before. And yet I can't figure out what it is I feel. All I know is I've shared more with Zach in twenty-four hours than I've shared with any other man in twenty-four months. With anyone ever. I'm usually very cautious when it comes to men."

"Zach's usually damn cautious when it comes to women. But I see the way he looks at you...." He rubbed his chin. "He tell you about Eileen?"

"Not in so many words. He didn't seem very broken up by her phone message calling it off."

Joe pulled his plate back and broke off a piece of cake with his fork. He didn't appear surprised. "Yeah, I knew that wouldn't last. Nice girl, too."

"And Cheryl? Was she nice?" Rebecca asked.

The piece of cake was making its way to Joe's mouth. He stopped midway and squinted at her. "Cheryl? Nice?" He gave it some thought before answering. "I guess. Some of the time, anyway."

"Zach said they fought a lot, that she couldn't handle the pressure of being married to someone who was always in the line of fire."

Joe quirked a smile. "The line of fire. Yeah. Truer words—"

"Is that what they fought about?"

Joe stopped smiling, his guard up. "That was part of it."

"What else?" she persisted.

"You know the kinds of things couples fight about," he hedged.

"No, I don't. I've never been part of a couple in that way. The closest I ever came to marriage was accepting a proposal from my seventh-grade boyfriend. He dumped me a month later for Alice Dickerson."

Joe looked dubious. "I'd have thought you'd be showered with marriage proposals twenty-four hours a day."

"Not from anyone who mattered to me." She pulled her chair up closer to the table. "Come on, Joe. What did they fight about besides Zach's work?"

"Oh, stuff. Money, chores, kids…"

"Kids? I thought there were no kids."

"There aren't."

"Didn't Zach want kids?" she pressed.

"Sure, he did."

"Then it was Cheryl? She didn't want children?"

"Look, I don't know. Zach didn't really confide in me. And I never spent much time with Cheryl. Maybe she just wasn't ready." Joe shifted uncomfortably in his chair. "I shouldn't be telling stories out of school."

"If you won't talk to me about him, who will? Zach holds everything inside. One of these days he could explode."

Joe gave her a long, penetrating look. "You might be the lit match that sets off the fuse."

8

THE CALL CAME IN AT six-fifteen in the morning. Zach was instantly alert. Years of practice. He grabbed up the phone. No one called this early unless it was bad news. The only question was what kind.

The second Zach heard Father Frank's voice, he knew. It was about the kid. Todd.

"He's gone," Father Frank said.

Zach's free hand clenched into a fist. He blamed himself. He shouldn't have left Todd at the shelter after getting that phone call from him. Maybe the kid hadn't gotten much of a look at the torch, but the torch couldn't be sure of that.

"When?" Zach gave none of his guilt and rage away in his tone of voice. There wasn't even any sign of it on his face. Only that clenched fist, the knuckles going white.

"I'm not sure," Father Frank said somberly. "None of the other boys in the dorm heard anything during the night. When the wake-up gong sounded at six... Todd's bed was empty."

"You didn't get a call from the hospital last night? Nothing about a change in Jerry's condition?"

"No. No word at all from the hospital. You think Todd could have been so worried about his brother that he went over there?"

Did Zach think so? No. Did he hope so? With all his heart. "I'll check with them first thing. Did you call the police yet?" Zach asked.

"Not yet. I called you first," the priest said.

There was a brief pause. "He probably just ran away, Zach. Kids like that—"

"Yeah, I know. Thanks, Father Frank. I'll be over there soon."

"Should I call the police or will you?"

"I will," Zach said. He had a few choice words to say to Lieutenant Lou Denehy over the phone. Whom had he chosen for the surveillance? Two new recruits still wet behind the ears?

"COME ON, ZACH. My boys did the best they could. They aren't perfect. This isn't a perfect world," Denehy said wearily.

"Tell me about it."

"What about the hospital? Could he have gone to his brother?"

"No. I just checked." Zach had known it was too good to be true. He shivered, thinking of how cheerful the nurse had sounded when she told him Jerry was doing so well. How well would he be doing after he heard about his kid brother...?

"I'll speak to my boys, Zach. After that I'll get right over there and look around, talk to some of the kids, see if I can pick up any clues."

"I'll meet you there."

MILLIE ROLLED OVER IN the bed as Joe hung up the phone. She squinted at the alarm clock. It was almost six-thirty.

Joe was getting out of bed. For all his bulk, he moved with a distinct quickness and agility whenever there was a call to duty.

"What happened, Joe?"

"The kid's missing from the shelter. Zach thinks the torch might have..." Joe let the sentence trail off. He didn't have the heart to finish it.

Millie didn't need to hear any more. "Oh, Joe," she said softly, putting a hand on his shoulder.

He gave her hand a squeeze. "I gotta go, honey."

"What about Rebecca?"

Joe looked over his shoulder at his wife. "Maybe you could teach her to bake cookies or something today. Anything to keep her out of Zach's hair. He's like a time bomb right now. I could hear the tick, tick, tick over the line."

WHEN REBECCA'S ALARM went off at seven-fifteen, the last thing in the world she wanted to do was get up and get out of bed. Thanks to all those early-morning wake-up calls when she was filming, however, she had trained herself to shake off exhaustion and answer her "call to duty."

She shivered when she tossed off the covers. It was cold in the room. She wrapped one of the blankets around her as she got out of bed. Looking out the frost-covered window she saw a solid curtain of gray clouds. Ice clung to the branches of the old elm outside the Kellys' house. A far cry from sunny Malibu.

When she opened the door of her bedroom and stepped into the hall she almost collided with Joe Junior who was coming out of the bathroom next door. He blushed a deep red.

"I didn't wake you, did I? Mom would have my head. I tried to be real quiet. Abbie and I are both finished with the...bathroom, so you can...have it as long as...you want."

Rebecca smiled. "Thanks. And don't worry. You didn't wake me. I've got to be up anyway. I'm leaving with your dad at eight-thirty for work."

"You are? Gee, my dad..."

"Joey," Millie called from the bottom of the stairs. "Your breakfast is getting cold."

Joe Junior gave Rebecca a wry smile, some of the rosiness fading from his cheeks. "I eat cold cereal for breakfast."

Rebecca was downstairs by eight-ten. She was wearing jeans, a black turtleneck sweater and boots, but she'd packed her sneakers in her tote bag in case she and Zach were going to be doing more digging in the burned-out building.

Millie was at the stove when Rebecca stepped into the kitchen.

"I hope you like bacon and eggs," Millie said brightly. "I should have asked you last night what you like for breakfast. You're so nice and trim, you probably don't eat all that much, but this being your first morning with us, and it being so cold and grim outside, I thought I'd make something hearty. I've even got fresh popovers. My mother's recipe. If you want a copy... But you probably don't cook much. Still, they're so easy. Take only a few minutes to whip up—"

"Where's Joe? Has he eaten yet?" Rebecca broke in.

"Oh, Joe and Abbie ate a while ago," Millie said, removing strips of cooked bacon from the pan and spreading them on paper toweling on the counter beside the stove. "They've got to be at school by eight. Now, how do you like your eggs? Scrambled? Sunnyside over? Or I could make you a cheese omelet. I've got some marvelous Vermont Cheddar cheese in the fridge. Have you ever had real Vermont Cheddar? Do they have a California Cheddar?"

"Millie, what's going on? Where's Joe? Joe Senior."

Millie smoothed back her hair. "He left early."

"What?"

"Don't be angry, Rebecca. It was an emergency. He dashed out of the house before seven."

Rebecca's heart started to pound. "What kind of an emergency? Another...fire?"

Millie began breaking eggs into a stainless-steel mixing bowl. "Oh, no. Not another fire."

"Then what?" Rebecca demanded.

Millie started beating the eggs. "I'm going to make you that Cheddar-cheese omelet, Rebecca. It's really one of my specialties."

Rebecca crossed the room and approached Millie. "Please tell me what's going on. Does it have something to do with Zach? Was it his idea that Joe sneak out without me?"

Millie gave Rebecca a sharp look. "He didn't sneak out. He got a call and threw his clothes on and ran out. Even if he had woken you up, you'd never have been ready—"

"Ready for what?"

Millie began beating the eggs harder. "Would you get the Cheddar cheese out of the fridge for me? There's a nice big wedge right in the cheese bin on the door."

"Millie, if you don't tell me what's going on, I'm going to walk right over to that phone and call the fire commissioner. Mr. Fitzgerald and I are like that," she said, holding up two crossed fingers.

Millie blanched. She stopped beating the eggs. "Stay here with me today, Rebecca. For Zach's sake."

"So, this emergency does have to do with Zach." Her skin suddenly turned clammy. "Something hasn't happened to him? The torch hasn't—"

"Zach's fine," Millie said, not quite meeting Rebecca's eyes.

"No, he isn't. Something is wrong." Millie was lying. She was a terrible actress. Rebecca could see right through her. Something was wrong. And it did involve Zach.

Rebecca leaned heavily against the counter, staring into the bowl of foaming eggs, feeling immobilized by the terrifying thoughts assaulting her mind.

"It's the boy," Millie said softly, seeing the actress's stricken look.

Rebecca's gaze darted to the older woman's face. "Jerry? The boy in the hospital? Oh, God, he hasn't—"

Millie's hand sprang out and she clasped Rebecca's arm. "No. No, not Jerry. His brother."

"Todd?" Rebecca was puzzled.

"He…disappeared from the shelter."

"Disappeared? You mean ran away?"

Millie sidestepped her and went to retrieve the cheese from the fridge herself. "I don't know exactly," she mumbled.

"Do you have a car?" Rebecca asked.

"Yes, but—"

"Where are they? Down at the shelter? Do you know where it is?"

Millie closed the refrigerator door. "Please stay here, Rebecca. Joe honestly thinks it would be for the best."

Rebecca wasn't listening. "Zach must feel sick with worry. And, knowing him, he feels completely responsible, as well."

A faint smile played on Millie's lips. "You are getting to know him, aren't you?"

"I guess I am. Can I borrow your car, Millie?"

"What about your breakfast?"

"Save it for me. I'll have it for dinner."

"At least try one of my popovers. And a cup of coffee. Or do you prefer tea? I have herbal tea if you don't like caffeine. Or plain tea." She scurried over to a cupboard. "I even think I've got some English breakfast tea my sister brought back from London last year. Then again, I don't know how long tea lasts. If it gets stale—"

"What aren't you telling me, Millie?" Rebecca interrupted. She was getting to know Joe Kelly's wife pretty well, too.

Millie wiped her hands on her apron. They didn't need wiping. "I don't know if you realize how dangerous this business can be. Every time Joe goes off, I get this…constriction in my chest. Even after all these years. It doesn't loosen up until I hear his car pull into the drive in the evening. Sometimes he doesn't make it back all night. I never really sleep then. Not a deep sleep. I can't. The fires are bad enough. That's not the worst of it, though."

"You mean the arsonists," Rebecca said softly.

"Some of them are just after the insurance money. Landlords and the like. Some are reckless kids out for a thrill. Some of them, though, are sick, demented souls. I still remember that gruesome man who burned down the Drake Hotel a few years back. The last of many fires he'd started that year. I went to the trial. It was the first time I did. I had to see him in person, even though Joe wasn't the least ways happy about it."

"Why did you have to see him?" Rebecca asked.

Millie stared off into space. "He'd invaded our lives. He'd come between me and Joe. When there's an arsonist on the loose like that, tracking him down becomes more than a job. It consumes you twenty-four hours a day. It was like that monster was living with us, taking away some of the very air we breathed. It was the same for Zach."

"Maybe even harder for him. Joe had you."

Millie nodded. "Poor Zach. Cheryl had left him just a few weeks earlier. Then that rescue, the accident. He was never the same. Oh, not just the limp. It was as if a light went out in him. He should have quit like he'd threatened. Or at least left Boston. Too many painful memories here. A change would have been good for him."

Millie smiled. "Zach, however, rarely does what's good for him. He's too busy driving himself to do what's right. He went to that trial every day, sat there right next to me, his eyes almost never straying from that torch."

"What did he look like? The torch?"

Millie smiled ruefully. "He looked so...ordinary. Average height, average weight, short-trimmed brown hair. A regular person you'd pass by on the street, never giving him a second look. That was what surprised me. Joe told me later, they usually do look ordinary."

"Maybe they look it on the outside," Rebecca said quietly. "But there's nothing ordinary about them on the inside. I haven't seen the one they're after now, but I heard his voice."

Millie hesitated. "Rebecca, Zach's worried that he might have...gone after...the boy."

Rebecca took in Millie's words in stunned silence. It was like a knife piercing her chest, filling her body with pain and terror. Not the boy. Not the child she, herself, had saved. She hadn't realized until that moment how deep a connection to him she felt. She remembered so vividly how his small body had clung to her in fear; how she'd rubbed his back, whispered soothing words to him, promising him he'd be okay. And she'd kept her word. He'd survived.

Tears spilled from Rebecca's eyes. Survived for what? An even more gruesome fate?

"Here, sit down," Millie was telling her gently. "I'll get you some tea and something to put in your stomach."

Rebecca stared at her through her haze of tears. "No. No, I've got to go. Please, Millie..."

The older woman nodded, leaving her to rummage through her black purse for her car keys. Without further distractions or preamble, she gave Rebecca directions to the shelter. As Rebecca was putting on her parka and starting for the kitchen door, Millie wrapped a still-warm popover in a paper napkin for her to eat on her drive over.

LIEUTENANT LOU DENEHY was a tall, gaunt man with a craggy, lined face and unruly black hair. Rubbing his icy hands together, he gave Zach and Joe a grim look. "My boys didn't see anyone lurking about the place and none of the kids here seem to have seen or heard anything."

Zach nodded. He, too, had spoken with the six boys in Todd's dorm, as well as the dozen or so other children being housed at the shelter. If the torch had snuck in and abducted Todd, he'd managed to do so without disturbing a soul.

Zach had tagged along with the two policemen Denehy had brought over to conduct the search. There were no overt signs of a struggle. Nothing of the boy's had been left behind, but then all he'd come there with were the clothes he had on his back, and the pajamas given to him, compliments of the shelter. The boy who'd slept next to Todd said that he'd slept with everything on. "Probably afraid one of us would rip him off," his dorm mate had said blasély.

All entries were checked. No doors or windows had been broken into, but one of the windows in the hallway outside the second-floor dorm was unlocked. Father Frank confessed that he believed some of the older children occasionally snuck in and out of the shelter late at night through this route, and any one of them might have been the culprit the previous night. A short trip along a wide ledge, and then all that was required was an easy slide down or a shimmy up the drainpipe. When the kids were questioned again, none of them would admit to having used that means of exit or entry the night before.

Joe cornered a harried, edgy Zach out in the hall. "I don't think this is going to get us anywhere."

"No, I suppose not," Zach said wearily, lighting a cigarette.

"I've got to fill in Collins. You shouldn't hang around here much longer."

"Yeah, I know...."

A commotion at the front door made them both turn around to find Rebecca arguing with the uniformed cop who had been posted there.

"No, I don't have any credentials on me," Rebecca was saying, and then she caught sight of Zach and Joe. She pointed to them. "They'll vouch for me."

Joe nodded to the cop, even as he heard Zach cursing under his breath.

"I did my best, Zach. Guess you can't keep a good woman down," Joe offered his partner as apology.

Zach glared at him, and as Rebecca rushed up to them, he bestowed the same look, only more intense, on her. "What are you doing here?"

Rebecca was in no mood for his outrage. "Did you find out anything?"

Zach turned on his heel and started off for the priest's office. Rebecca reached out and grabbed his arm. "Damn it, Zach. I have a right to know. I'm a part of this. You can't shut me out."

He spun on her, dark eyes glinting. "Is that from one of your movie scripts? What are we playing here? Righteous indignation? You're good, sweetheart. Real good. Now, me—I'm winging it. That's what we do in the real world. Nobody hands us any lines. We don't say the right things at the right times. We don't do the right things even if we're trying. Sometimes we screw it up. Sometimes we screw it up royally. No second takes. And you being here is only making it worse...."

Joe put a meaty hand on Zach's shoulder. "Take it easy, kid. We're all of us pretty worked up now. No point in blaming ourselves or each other."

Zach shrugged off Joe's hand and stormed off. Rebecca gave Joe a wan look.

"It's killing him, isn't it?"

Joe nodded. "He got a call from the kid last night." Joe gave her a brief rundown, although for the life of him he didn't know why he was filling her in. Maybe it was because she'd been the one to find that button that could well turn out to be a clue to the torch. Maybe it was because she'd been the one to carry Todd out of that burning building. Maybe it was because it was as clear as rain to him that Rebecca Fox was nuts about his partner. And just as clear, for all Zach's surliness, that he was nuts about her.

Rebecca forced herself to listen to Joe without interruption or panic, neither of which was easy.

"It's possible, still, that the kid just took off," Joe finished. "We've got no proof that the torch got to him."

Rebecca looked past Joe to the priest's closed office door where Zach had disappeared. "So what do we do now?"

Joe shrugged. "There's not much we can do. The police are in on it now. They've got an all-points bulletin out on the kid."

"If something terrible's happened to Todd, Zach's never going to forgive himself. Even though he did what he could."

"I know that and you know that, but Zach..." Joe smiled crookedly. "You eat anything this morning?"

Rebecca shook her head. Millie's wrapped-up popover, much deflated, was still in her jacket pocket.

"There's a coffee shop across the street. I'll buy you a cup of coffee and some waffles. You like waffles?"

"What about Zach?"

"He hates waffles."

Reluctantly, Rebecca let Joe lead her out of the shelter.

AS SHE DISTRACTEDLY nibbled on her waffle, Rebecca's gaze kept shifting out the window of the coffee shop to the shelter across the street. She saw an unmarked car pull up to the curb. At the same time, she heard a low grunt from Joe who was sitting across from her in the booth, nursing a cup of coffee.

"Who is it?"

Joe was rising from the bench. "Collins. Our boss. If he runs into Zach in there, he'll blow a gasket."

Joe had barely finished the sentence when they saw Zach come out the shelter's front door, practically running smack-dab into the bureau chief. From her vantage point, Rebecca could see the two men stare at each other in tense silence for a couple of moments and then both began shouting at once. It wasn't necessary to read lips to guess what they were saying.

Joe was throwing some money on the table. "I'd better get out there and try to smooth things out."

Rebecca started to rise, but Joe motioned her back down. "If Collins sees you here, too, it will only go harder for Zach."

Rebecca nodded, knowing Joe was probably right. She sat back down, even pulling the red-and-white gingham café curtain across the window so that if Collins glanced over at the coffee shop he wouldn't spot her.

Joe smiled and took off.

Peeking through the slit in the curtain, Rebecca watched Joe dash across the street. Zach and Collins were still in their verbal fighting match and it looked at first like Joe was having a hard time getting a word in edgewise. After a couple of minutes, though, Rebecca was relieved to see that Joe managed to catch the chief's ear. Zach stood there glaring at both of them.

"I DON'T HAVE TIME FOR this," Zach cut in sharply as Joe—lying like a pro—was explaining to Collins that he had to take the heat since he was the one who had called Zach to come down to the shelter.

Zach headed across the street.

"Where are you going?" Collins called out.

Zach stopped abruptly in the middle of the road, forcing an oncoming cab to do a quick maneuver around him. "Where am I going? On vacation," he shouted over the angry blare of the cabbie's horn. "I've got almost three weeks coming to me. So, I'm out of here."

"You trying to pull something, Zach?" Collins shouted back. "You go messing with this case while you're off duty and—"

"And speaking about being on vacation—" Zach cut him off "—this means you're going to have to find some other tour guide for your Hollywood glamour girl."

"Now, hold on," Collins called out, starting after Zach only to be pulled back onto the curb by Joe a second before a Boston tour bus rolled over his toes.

By the time the bus passed, Zach was out of sight.

REBECCA GRABBED THE MENU wedged between the stainless-steel napkin holder and the jukebox, threw it open and hid behind it as Zach stormed into the coffee shop. Peering cautiously over the top of the menu, she saw Zach head straight for a phone. He dialed and listened, saying nothing, his features grim.

She realized he must be calling into his answering machine to see if the torch, or hopefully Todd, had left any messages. From the brief length of time he kept the receiver to his ear and the way he slammed the receiver down on the hook, she doubted there'd been any messages at all. Certainly not any good ones.

As she watched Zach head for the front door, Rebecca lowered the menu from her face. Just then, a waitress came over to her table and exclaimed excitedly, "Aren't you Rebecca Fox? Oh, my God, I can't believe it. It is you. Look everyone, Rebecca Fox." All eyes in the coffee shop turned to her. Including Zach's.

Rebecca's gaze locked with his for a moment before he stalked out. In that brief instant, she saw in him exactly what she was feeling inside—the fear, the anguish, the apprehension that he was fighting so hard to mask. It was a glimpse into his soul. And a connection with him that was stronger than the passion they'd experienced the other night. A connection so strong it took her breath away.

"I'VE ALREADY TOLD the police and the arson investigator that Jerry's brother has not been to the hospital since yesterday morning when Jerry was operated on," the nurse said, her patience wearing thin. The large-boned woman with a furrowed face and heavy jowls had already gone through several rounds of questioning that morning.

Rebecca nodded sympathetically. "I guess I was hoping that maybe he'd snuck in without anyone spotting him. I remember one time when my mom was in the hospital. Appendicitis. I was eleven and the hospital had this rule that no one under thirteen could visit without an adult. I was heading home from school and I'd gotten this great grade on a composition and I was sure my mom would be so happy to see it. So I snuck up to her room and when the nurse came in, I ducked into her closet...." It was a bald-faced lie, but she was proud of her performance.

The nurse folded her arms across her starched white uniform. "Are you saying you'd like me to check Jerry's closet?"

"Could you?"

The nurse squinted up at her. "You look very familiar. Have I ever seen you here before? Or somewhere else? I pride myself on always placing a face...."

Rebecca, her face hidden behind the new pair of oversize black-rimmed glasses she'd picked up on the way over to the hospital, gave the nurse a blank look. "It's possible, I guess. I've lived over in Dorchester for the last fifteen years. Are you from Dorchester?"

"No," the nurse said. "Charlestown."

"I have a cousin who lives in Charlestown. Sam…Porter." She hid a smile as she thought of the face her agent would make at the very idea of residing anywhere but L.A.

"I know a Phil Porter. Owns the dry-cleaning store over on Sargeant Street."

Rebecca pondered that for a couple of seconds, then shook her head, returning to the issue at hand. "What do you say?" she asked, a note of pleading in her voice. "Would you give Jerry's room a once-over? On the chance Todd is hiding in there?"

The nurse shrugged. "All right. But I'm sure he isn't in there. I've been in and out of that room all morning, and—"

"Please."

The nurse shuffled off, returning two minutes later. She held her hands out, palms up. "I told you.…"

For good measure, Rebecca looked into the janitor's closet on her way over to the elevator, and even checked out the empty doctors' lounge, looking under the sofa, behind the television console. No Todd.

Riding down in the elevator, she hugged herself against a chill that had nothing to do with the nasty December weather. She stepped into the lobby, which was festively decorated for Christmas. She sighed heavily. This was going to be a Christmas to remember. For all the wrong reasons.

After leaving the hospital, Rebecca was at a loss for where to go next. Back to the office? The thought of Collins attaching her to another investigator now that Zach was "on vacation" didn't exactly lift her spirits. She didn't want to be attached to another partner. She was already far too attached to the one she had.

WHEN REBECCA TURNED down Zach's street, she saw his beat-up Ford parked along the curb in front of the charred remains of the boarded-up town house. Was

Zach in there, doing another search? Did he think that possibly the torch had returned, Todd in tow, to the scene of the crime?

Stepping out of her car, she hesitated in front of the burned-out building. Should she continue on her own hunt? She was desperate to find the child, as desperate as she knew Zach was to find him. If any harm had come to that kid... If that torch had kidnapped him and done something heinous...

Her breath jammed in her throat. She'd played desperation in some of her films. She'd played fear, panic. Now she was experiencing what all of those emotions were *really* like. A far cry from the ones she'd fabricated for the camera.

Something stirred in the shadows of the charred shell. Ignoring the roped-off area, Rebecca ducked underneath the barrier, edging closer to the building.

"Zach? Zach, are you in there?" Her voice sounded unnaturally low as she called out to him.

There was no response, no further movement.

If Zach was in there, it was possible he wouldn't answer her. Possible? Hell, probable. Hadn't he spelled it out to her? To Joe? To Collins? To Fitzgerald? He wanted her out of his hair, out of his life.

"Zach, we've got to talk." She inched closer to the building, trying to convince herself it was Zach skulking around in there because if it wasn't Zach, she could be walking right into the arms of a madman.

"I'm not so easy to get rid of, Zach. I don't know what it is about me, but I always have to finish what I've started. So, if you're on vacation, so am I. I'm on vacation with you, Zach."

She gingerly made her way over the rubble to what had once been the lobby. "Call it a baptism of fire, Zach. That's what happened to me. To us. It's a bond now, no matter how much you want to deny it."

A distant rustling sound stopped her cold. Maybe

this wasn't such a good idea. Surely Zach wouldn't stay silent, letting her muck about in there and risk getting hurt. He cared too much, even if he didn't know it yet. Or want to know it.

She stared into the dark cavity of the building, little chills rippling down her back. What if the noise she'd heard was Todd? Todd, lying helpless, possibly trussed up in the ruins? If it was Todd, was he likely to be alone? Or was this yet another kind of trap set by the insidious arsonist?

Rebecca closed her eyes, her mind whirring, her bravery slowly but surely evaporating. She couldn't get herself to go and investigate. Still, she couldn't get herself to leave the building, either. She felt paralyzed by fear and indecision.

A creaking sound made her heart leap. Instinctively, she shut her eyes. Someone—something—scurried past her, brushing against her legs. Her eyes sprang open.

She gave a nervous little laugh. A cat. A black cat. Good thing she wasn't superstitious.

HE SMILED, HIDDEN FROM her by a large partially-charred support beam. She was close enough so that he could pick up her scent, even though the air in there was still heavy with the smell of smoke and blistering, burning wood and plaster.

He liked her scent. He liked the way she looked. He'd never had a woman like her. What was it she'd said about a "baptism by fire"?

His smile deepened. Chapin hadn't been the only one to share that with her. He'd shared it with her, too. It was a bond now, a bond connecting all three of them. Their first shared baptism by fire. But not their last.

this went back around her slowly. Zach would have been silent, letting her much abler to desire and the meaning part. He cared too much, even that didn't know if you love, or hadn't yet.

She turned into the hallway of the building, strip...

be very confident to step inside, people passed as the the halls. If it was back, was on back, to be

9

REBECCA TOOK HEAPING gulps of fresh air as she stepped back out into the street. Her gaze rested on Zach's building, her expression thoughtful as she absently spun her gold-and-ruby ring around her finger. She had to see Zach, talk to him, get him to see that they had unfinished business—professional and personal— to settle.

She crossed the street, determination in her step. Her resolve diminished the closer she got to his building. He probably wouldn't even let her inside his apartment. And if he did, she knew that a direct confrontation would only cause Zach to retreat even further.

She was still nervously twisting that ring around her finger as the idea struck. Quickly she removed the ring, tucking it into one of the deep front pockets of her jeans.

She rang his buzzer. No response. No surprise. Good thing she'd made another friend in the building.

A minute after ringing the superintendent's buzzer, he appeared at the door.

He winked at her, asking no questions. The newspaper article had made it clear she wasn't Zach's "cousin." She made a dash for the elevator, pressing Zach's floor.

She was nervous as she rapped loudly on his door. "Zach, it's me. Rebecca. Listen, please let me in. I lost my ring. I think it might have fallen off my finger when I was sleeping on your couch. The ring means a lot to me, Zach. It has...sentimental value." She didn't even remember who had given it to her.

She stared in frustration at the closed door. "Damn it, Zach."

The elevator doors slid open. The superintendent walked out. As he came down the hall toward her the ring of keys on his belt jangled.

"He must be asleep. I misplaced my ring. I don't suppose you could—"

"Only if you promise to keep your word about stopping down to see my wife later. She's due home from work at three."

"I'm looking forward to it," Rebecca lied with the earnestness of an accomplished actress.

The superintendent inserted his spare key into the lock and Rebecca slipped inside Zach's apartment. As she closed the door behind her she steeled herself for the anticipated confrontation. Zach didn't appear. As she moved cautiously into the living room, she found it empty. She called to him, but there was no response. The kitchen door was open, and she could see from where she was standing that it, too, was empty. Had Zach gone out for a fresh pack of cigarettes? Or some more fast food? His car was out front so he couldn't have gone far. She was on the way to check the bedroom, when the phone rang. Her hand sprang up to her heart. What if it was the torch? What if he was calling to tell Zach about a new fire? Or about Todd? By the third ring, Rebecca knew she had to pick up. She started across the living room for the phone.

ZACH WAS SHAMPOOING his hair under the hot, steamy spray when he heard a faint ringing sound. Ignoring the soapsuds running down his face, he shut off the water, recognizing the distinct ring of the telephone. He sprang out of the shower, skidding across the slippery tiles on the bathroom floor, and was about to answer the extension in the bedroom when it stopped ringing.

Cursing under his breath, he rubbed away the soap-suds dripping down from his hair onto his face. Shivering, he started back for the shower, when a familiar voice in the next room stopped him cold.

Forgetting his state of dress—or undress as it was in this case—Zach strode into the living room, dumb-founded to find Rebecca in rapt conversation on his telephone.

"I CAN'T BELIEVE THIS. This is so wonderful. You don't know how—" Rebecca stopped abruptly as she saw Zach standing there, his hair covered in shampoo, without a stitch on. She stared at him stunned. And instantly aroused.

Zach demanded to know what she was doing back in his apartment again, taking calls on his phone, no less, when it hit him that his appearance had startled Rebecca as much as her appearance had startled him. Talk about feeling exposed.

"It's…Gail," Rebecca muttered inanely.

Zach's hands dropped discreetly in front of him. He could feel his face turning beet red. "Gail?"

Rebecca tried not to stare. She wasn't successful. "My…personal manager."

"Oh, that's just great. Now you've got your personal manager phoning you over here—"

"No, Zach. You don't understand. She didn't phone me. She was phoning you, looking for me."

"I don't exactly see—"

She broke into a wide smile. "It's about Todd. He's with Gail."

His nudity forgotten, Zach sped across the room and grabbed the phone out of Rebecca's hand.

"What's the story?" he barked.

"Hi," Gail chirped at the other end of the line. "Zach, I presume."

"Is Todd with you?" He turned his back to Rebecca, but he could feel her eyes boring into him.

"Yes, he's here."

"Where's here?"

"The Heritage. Rebecca's suite."

"I don't get it. Is he okay? Let me speak to him."

Rebecca took the receiver from him. "Gail told me he's fast asleep, Zach. We'll go over there later." She put the phone to her ear. "Thanks, Gail. I'll see you in a couple of hours." She dropped the receiver into the cradle. Then slowly, blatantly, she let her eyes cruise down Zach's glistening-wet, naked body. In the heat of passion the other night, she hadn't noticed the web of scars running down his left hip and leg, which she guessed was a souvenir of the Drake fire. She felt a wave of sadness that in no way diminished her attraction to him. If anything, it heightened it.

"You certainly do have a knack for popping in unexpectedly," Zach said dryly.

"I did knock first."

"I was in the shower."

She grinned. "You still have soap in your hair."

"Why'd you come back?"

She dug her hand in her pocket. "To search for this ring I was going to tell you I lost in your sofa."

A faint smile played on his lips.

Rebecca smiled, too. "Oh, Zach. Todd's okay. The torch didn't get him."

Zach was still a little dazed by the good news—not to mention Rebecca's surprise appearance. "It doesn't make any sense."

"Sure, it does," Rebecca said. "Todd probably got scared in the night and decided to come find me. All the papers said I was at the Heritage. Luckily, Gail was there when he showed up at eight-thirty this morning.

He'd been roaming the streets of Boston all night trying to find the hotel. He told Gail he wanted my autograph for his brother. Jerry's a big fan."

So am I, Zach was thinking, the relief of learning of Todd's safety finally sinking in. As was the chill. And something else. A pulsating desire he'd been fighting all day.

"You really ought to rinse that shampoo out of your hair or it's going to be very unmanageable," Rebecca murmured. But it wasn't his hair she was focusing on.

"Unmanageable, huh?"

"Very unmanageable," she reiterated.

Zach stared at her long and hard. "That's not the only 'very unmanageable' problem I have."

She responded with a provocative survey of his naked body. "You're not going to take me over your knee and spank me?"

He shook his head slowly as he advanced. "No. That wasn't exactly what I had in mind."

The next thing Rebecca knew, he'd swept her up in his arms and was carrying her off to the bathroom.

"What do you think you're doing?" she protested, albeit weakly.

"I've had my turn at show-and-tell. Now it's yours. Besides, I thought you wanted to try out the rest of the rooms in this place."

"I thought you weren't…interested."

"Any man in his right mind would be interested, Rebecca. Granted, I'm not always in my right mind. At the moment, my mind has gone to mush."

"Definitely not the rest of you," she replied playfully. Wasn't it wonderful, she thought, how one kid safely tucked away at the Heritage could transform her and Zach from warriors to lovers?

Once in the bathroom, Zach stepped right into the shower with her.

"But I'm…dressed!" she exclaimed.

He gave her a sly look as he turned the water back on. "Not for long."

She was soaked in seconds. "You know what this means, don't you?" she said, rubbing the water from her eyes.

He smiled, soapsuds running down his face. "It means we're hot for each other."

She smiled back. "That, too. It also means I'm stuck here until my clothes dry."

"There's a dryer in the basement," he said, pulling her sopping black sweater up over her head.

"The basement, huh?" Her words were muffled by the sweater being yanked off.

He flung the soaked garment over the shower-curtain rod. "You are wanton, Rebecca Fox."

"And you love it."

He was attacking the snap of her sodden jeans. Getting them off was going to be no easy feat. "Okay, I love it," he confessed, tugging.

She helped him out, tugging with him, rotating her hips against him as she did, heightening his already heightened arousal. And hers.

When she was down to her lacy black bra and black silk panties, he gave her a slow, provocative study. "Did you ever film a love scene in a shower?" he asked.

She shook her head slowly, her wet hair smelling of lavender and citrus.

The pads of his thumbs rubbed her hardened nipples through the wet cloth of her bra. She emitted a little gasp, pressing her lips to his shoulder, taking small, nibbling bites of his flesh.

"How about in real life?" he persisted, his palms sliding over her breasts to her stomach.

She looked up at him. "You want to know if this is a first for me? It's a first for me, Zach. Everything that's happening between us is a first for me. I think I'm falling in—"

His mouth clamped down hard over hers, cutting off the rest of what she needed to say to him; what he desperately did not want to hear. He could handle the physical intensity of their relationship. The emotional part was another matter altogether.

Rebecca kissed him back, the hot jets of water pulsating on her flesh. The words would keep for now, although she knew at some point they'd have to be said. Not that she was taking the realization of her feelings any better than he was likely to. Loving Zach wouldn't be easy under the best of circumstances. And these were far from the best.

Her hands moved along the planes of his torso, lingering on his scarred hip where her fingers gently followed the webbed pattern.

He placed his hand over hers. "Does it bother you?"

"No," she said truthfully. "They're part of what makes you who you are."

"Who am I?" Zach asked.

As she parted her lips to answer, he pressed a finger to them. "No, don't tell me. I'm not sure I want to know."

They kissed again, this time Zach's fingers releasing the snap of her bra. As their kiss deepened, he kneaded her breasts gently, pulling at her nipples, making her gasp with longing. She began her own intimate exploration, reveling in Zach's soft moans of pleasure. They were both feeling the same fiery urgency as they had the other night in his kitchen, but this time neither of them wanted it over fast. They wanted a chance to explore, caress, learn all the contours and curves of each other's bodies.

The shower was hot and steamy. Zach twined his fingers between Rebecca's, lifting her arms up over her head, pressing her against the cool, tiled wall. The contrast of hot and cold was tantalizing.

Wrapping one leg around him, she kept her arms extended as his fingers disappeared in her wet hair to massage her scalp, then followed the curve of her shoulders, moving slowly down her sides.

"That feels wonderful," she murmured breathlessly, pressing up against him, relishing the hot wetness of flesh against flesh. She wanted her body to dissolve into his. She imagined herself slipping through his skin, being wholly absorbed by him. She wanted to be a part of Zach. In so many ways they were a lot alike— brash, driven, determined, arrogant, defiant. In this short time with Zach, Rebecca realized she was also discovering new things about herself. Her daring, for one. For another, her capacity to feel more deeply for someone than she'd ever imagined possible. A third discovery was waiting in the wings—her capacity to hurt. The hurting time, she knew, was just around the corner. She pushed the knowledge of that pain aside, allowing only the pleasure to consume her. There would be time enough later for the other.

Dropping her arms, she encircled them around his neck, kissing him hard on the lips, her tongue darting into his mouth, her body arching into him.

"Oh, Zach, you set me on fire," she whispered, pressing her bruised lips against his ear.

"I'm burning up with you," Zach said raspily, pulling her fully under the pulsating jets of water.

She squeezed her eyes closed as he slowly lowered himself to his knees, his mouth cruising sinuously down her body. Gently but firmly, he pried her legs apart, as his mouth moved lower still.

She cried out as his moist, heated tongue and warm breath claimed her, his palms cupping her buttocks roughly. Her fingers dug into his scalp. Her whole body was afire; rockets were going off inside her. Her hips began to rotate of their own volition. She felt possessed as she was being possessed, all sensation gathered in the core of her.

When he finally rose and entered her, she was trembling like a leaf, crying out with abandon at every thrust, her wet hair tangling with his, her long legs wrapped fully around him now. His hands were under her buttocks to support her as he pressed her against the tile wall, plunging deeper and deeper into her. It felt to Zach like they were connecting from the inside out instead of the reverse.

Rebecca was dissolving into the wetness and the steam. She could feel Zach inside her, hard and quivering, like a second heartbeat. Tears stung her eyes as her orgasm came, exploding, shattering.

"Oh, Zach, I love you...so...much."

Zach opened his mouth to respond, but only a hoarse cry of release came out; the words, as well as the feelings, were strangled deep in his throat.

REBECCA LAY BESIDE ZACH afterward on his double bed. Her hand rested lightly on his bare chest. He was about to reach for a cigarette on the bedside table, then reconsidered. Rebecca smiled, placing a tender kiss of approval on his cheek.

"I've been meaning to quit for months," he muttered.

"Now, if you gave up the junk food, as well..."

He shot her a look.

"Okay, okay. Forget the junk food."

He couldn't forget. Not any of it. That was the problem.

There was a long silence. Rebecca knew it would be longer still if she waited for Zach to speak. It wasn't easy, though, at center stage without a script, winging it.

"Zach, lots of people work out long-distance relationships. We could—"

"We're not lots of people, Rebecca," he cut her off swiftly. The worst thing, Zach figured, was to have any illusions. Face it square on. Be realistic. Honest.

He drew her away from him. Eye-to-eye contact. God, she had such beautiful eyes. Chocolate brown with glints of gold. It was going to be hell letting her go.

"This will be great while it lasts, Rebecca, but let's not delude ourselves. It's going to be over in a few weeks. Less still if you change your mind and go back sooner." His words gave no hint of his inner feelings, his inner turmoil. They should never have begun this, but he knew that was like saying he should never have taken his first breath.

"I'm not going to go back sooner, Zach," she said stubbornly. "Right now I don't feel like ever going back," she confessed.

"What are you saying? You'd give up your fabulous movie career, this picture of a lifetime you want so badly, your fancy L.A. digs, your glitzy friends, everything, to move into this crummy apartment with me, bake cookies while I'm off tracking down arsonists...?"

"I could be your partner for real."

He shook his head at her as though she were a silly child. "I'd better go throw your clothes in the dryer downstairs. We should get over to the hotel soon."

He started to get out of bed, but Rebecca grabbed his arm. "Okay, it wouldn't work," she said wanly. "I don't want to give up my career. It's important to me." She sat up, too, pressing her chest into his back. "But you're important to me, too, Zach. It doesn't seem fair to have to choose."

His features hardened. "Who said life is fair? You think Todd or Jerry think it's fair? You think that poor bum that got fried to a crisp thinks it's fair? You think I do?"

She hesitated. "You could...come out to L.A. with me. Fitzgerald says you've been talking about quitting for years."

"And what do you suggest I do? Swim laps in your swank pool and shop on Rodeo Drive while you're off playing love scenes with some movie-star hunk? I don't think so, sweetheart. That's not my scene. And this isn't yours."

"Oh, Zach…"

He turned around and put his arms around her, holding her against his bare chest. "This probably was a real dumb idea," he murmured in a sad, regretful voice.

"I don't know," Rebecca said, determined not to let reality undermine the pleasure they'd shared. "I can think of worse ways of starting off a vacation."

He kissed her softly on the lips. "I'm afraid the vacation's over, baby." He held her tight. "Let's quit while we're ahead. I've already got enough scar tissue to last a lifetime. And you don't want any of your own, believe me." His voice was tender yet distant.

A short while ago when Zach had held her in his arms, Rebecca had felt so close to him. Now, even as she clung to him, she felt an ever-widening chasm— Zach having once again resurrected his handy-dandy invisible but impenetrable wall.

ZACH DROVE A ROUNDABOUT route to the hotel, wanting to make sure they weren't being followed. The arsonist might not know Todd's whereabouts, but he certainly knew where his favorite arson investigator lived. Rebecca, who didn't know the city very well, didn't suspect anything. Her mind was not on the arsonist at the moment. It was on Zach. Next week was Christmas, then came New Year's; and then she was gone. Would she ever see Zach again? If she did get the Paradisi part—which she was going to fight for tooth and nail after all this—she'd be involved in the making of the film for a good three months. No time for a getaway visit to Boston. Would Zach fly out to L.A. to see her? Certainly not if he was still after the torch. And once he was caught, there'd be another one. Always another one. He'd use his work as an excuse not to come out, but Rebecca knew the real reason would be that he'd find a brief reunion too painful. Not that it would be any different for her.

She was unaware of heaving a sigh until Zach reached out and tenderly rested a hand on her thigh. She placed her hand over his until he gently but resolutely drew his hand back to the steering wheel.

"I've got to come up with a new plan for Todd. I don't think the shelter's such a good idea," Zach said, determined to keep his mind focused on business.

"You mean it's too dangerous."

"How did you...?"

"Joe told me about Todd calling you. About his seeing the arsonist. Which means the arsonist might have spotted him."

Zach frowned. "It's not like Joe to go running off at the mouth."

"Don't take it out on him, Zach. It's not Joe you're mad at," she said quietly.

He didn't say anything, but his frown deepened.

"I don't know, Zach. Maybe if you hadn't popped out of your bedroom stark naked... Maybe if we weren't both a little punch-drunk hearing that Todd was safe... Maybe if it hadn't been so good the last time..."

Zach cut her off. "If I'm mad at anybody, it's myself. I knew where this was going. I could have not gone along for the ride."

"You tried."

He smiled. "Not very hard. You've never seen me when I'm really trying hard."

Rebecca stared at him somberly. "I'm seeing you now."

His smile vanished. He knew she was right.

They drove the rest of the way to the hotel in silence, both of them feeling a numbness settle in. The slight dampness still clinging to Rebecca's jeans despite twenty minutes in the dryer were her only reminder that the steamy passion she and Zach had shared in the shower such a short time ago wasn't an illusion.

As THEY CROSSED the hotel lobby, Rebecca could see that Zach was on the alert. She stepped closer to him, her own senses heightened.

"You don't think he followed us here?" she asked anxiously.

"I don't think so, but I can't be sure," Zach said grimly. "The thing to do is to get Todd away from here without being seen."

"Where do we take him?"

Zach didn't answer. For one thing, he hadn't figured that out yet. For another, they were approaching the elevator where several hotel guests were gathered. Zach's gaze took in each of them—two women and three men. The women, well-dressed and well-preserved, obviously knew each other. They were chatting together amiably. Two of the three men were middle-aged and very respectable looking. Business types. They sported tailored suits, shined shoes, and leather attaché cases. Each had a wool overcoat slung over his arm. The third man was younger and not nearly as well-dressed as the two older men. He was quite tall, very thin, with rounded shoulders from years of slouching. What really drew Zach's attention was the bulky navy blue raincoat the man was wearing.

As the elevator arrived, Zach held Rebecca back on the pretense of searching for something in his pocket. The others stepped in, then turned to face the doors. As the doors started to slide closed, Zach shot his hand out to reopen them. He motioned Rebecca in ahead of him.

There were no buttons missing on the man's raincoat. Not that that proved anything one way or the other.

Rebecca saw Zach's surreptitious shake of his head as she went to press the button for her floor. She immediately dropped her hand to her side, a tremor of fear zigzagging down her spine. She, too, had noticed the young man in the raincoat.

They both felt a rush of relief when he exited on the seventh floor. The women disembarked next on the eleventh, and the two men were both gone by the time they arrived on the nineteenth floor where Rebecca's suite was located.

Zach maintained his caution as they stepped out onto Rebecca's floor, nudging her behind him as they entered the long, opulent and, from what they could tell, empty hallway. Rebecca pointed to the end of the hall—suite 19B.

"I gave Gail my key," she said when they got to the door.

Zach knocked.

They stared straight ahead, waiting.

The wait was getting too long. Rebecca shot Zach an anxious look. He knocked again.

There was no response.

Rebecca gripped her hands together. "Gail could have gone out for something. Todd could still be sleeping."

Zach's bland expression gave no indication of the worry churning up inside him. Always cool under fire. *Almost* always.

"I'm going to go down and get the key."

"Oh, Zach. You don't think—"

He gave her arm a squeeze. "No point in thinking anything yet."

"Right," Rebecca said, but she couldn't help thinking. Any more than Zach could.

The few minutes it took Zach to return felt like an eternity.

"I kept knocking…just in case," Rebecca said, her voice raspy with concern.

Zach slipped the key in the lock. Before he turned it, he looked over at Rebecca. "Stay out here."

Her eyes widened with fear. "Oh, God," she whispered.

Zach wanted to give her some words of comfort, but he knew Rebecca was too smart to buy them. There was nothing to do but unlock the door, go in and face whatever there was to face.

Rebecca stood in the hall, clutching herself tightly, trying to still the trembling when Zach called out to her.

She stepped gingerly inside the door.

Zach was coming out of the bedroom. "No one's here. The bed's unmade and still warm."

"Do you think the torch…? Do you think he took them both?" Rebecca felt immeasurable guilt for having talked Gail into staying on at the suite. If she'd gone to stay with her parents as she'd planned…

"I looked around for a note. I didn't find one. Did Gail have a special place for putting them?"

Rebecca felt dazed. She shook her head dumbly only to find Zach steering her over to one of the print brocade settees in the parlor. "Sit down and take a few deep breaths. You're white as a sheet."

She did as he ordered, only then realizing that she was light-headed.

Zach crossed to the phone. He'd have to let the police know the latest developments. On the way over to the hotel he'd planned to phone them when he got here and tell them they could put that all-points bulletin on Todd on ice. Now it looked like they'd have to not only keep that one active, but add one more name. Gail…He realized he didn't even know Gail's last name.

He was about to ask Rebecca what it was when he saw two figures at the front door of the suite. He stared at them in stunned silence. One of them was Todd. The other he assumed was Gail. She was smiling brightly.

"Hi. I didn't expect you'd get here so fast," Gail said cheerily. "I took Todd down to the dining room for some lunch. You should have seen the size of the roast-beef sandwich he packed away."

Gail looked at the pair in the room, both of them frozen to their spots. She wore a perplexed expression. "What is it? What's wrong?" She zeroed in on Rebecca. "You look like you've just seen a ghost."

Rebecca sprang up from the settee, ran over to Gail and put her arms around her.

"Gail, Gail. I'm so glad to see you," Rebecca cried, hugging the surprised woman tightly.

Todd smiled awkwardly at Zach.

Zach grinned. "Actresses."

"I'M TELLING YOU it will be fine," Gail was insisting fifteen minutes later, despite Zach having taken her aside and warned her that the arsonist could well be on the lookout for Todd. Gail's response had been that he wasn't likely to find Todd at her family's home in Scituate, a coastal town about thirty miles south of the city.

"What do you think, Todd?" Zach asked. "Would you like to spend the Christmas holidays with Miss McCarthy?"

Todd was hesitant. "Well...I would... Only...what about Jerry?"

Zach put a comforting arm around Todd's shoulder. "Jerry's going to be in the hospital for a couple of weeks, kid. I'm sure he'd be happy to know you were with a nice family while he's recuperating."

"I'll make you a promise," Rebecca said to Todd. "I'll go over to the hospital on Christmas Day and celebrate with Jerry."

"Will you bring him an autographed picture?" Todd asked shyly.

"Yes. And some other stuff, too. Maybe some CDs. What groups does he like?"

Todd's cherubic face reddened. "He likes rap. Only...he doesn't have a CD player or...anything."

Rebecca smiled gently. "Well, now, Santa just might have one of those nifty portable CD players in his sack for Jerry."

Todd's green eyes widened. "Gee, he'd be blown away if he got that."

Zach tousled Todd's unruly brown hair, which was in dire need of a haircut. His heart went out to the waif. And to his older brother in the hospital. Zach would have liked to have a few choice words with the parents who'd abandoned these kids. Didn't they know that children were to be treasured?

As Rebecca watched Zach's gentle interaction with Todd, she remembered her late-night conversation with Joe about Zach having wanted children of his own. She wanted children, too. When she found the right guy. A sadness enveloped her. She and Zach could make some beautiful children together.

While Gail put in a phone call to her parents telling them to expect her and her young charge within the hour, Zach took Todd aside.

"Remember that guy you were telling me about on the phone, Todd?"

The boy nodded. "The one I saw outside just before the fire."

"Can you describe him for me?"

Todd pursed his lips and absently rapped his knuckles into his palm. "Not really. It was dark. He looked kind of...ordinary."

"Young? Old?"

"About like you, I guess."

Zach winked. "Old."

Todd blushed.

"Was he about my height? My size?" Zach pressed.

"I guess. Sort of. I couldn't really tell."

Zach nodded. "Yeah, it would be hard, especially looking down on him. You said he looked up at one point."

"Yeah, he did."

"Could you see his face at all, or was it too dark?"

"It was pretty dark, but..."

Zach smiled encouragingly.

"He had sort of a mean face."

"Mean?" Zach glanced over at Rebecca who was standing a few feet behind Todd. She approached the child.

"Did he look a little like this?" she asked, drawing her lips into a tight line and sucking in her cheeks.

At first Todd laughed, but as he continued looking at her contorted face, he began to nod. "Yeah. Kind of like that." He stared at her in awe. "Say, that's real good."

Rebecca smiled, her features shifting back into their right places. "It takes practice."

AFTER SEEING Todd and Gail safely off in a rented blue sedan, Zach turned to Rebecca. "How'd you know the kid saw a guy with a narrow face, sunken cheeks, and thin lips?"

"Todd said he looked mean. Most kids classify people from stereotypes from TV and the movies. Mean guys on the tube or the big screen usually have narrow faces, sunken cheeks and thin lips."

Zach opened the car door for her. "That's good. That's very good."

"Doesn't get us very far though, does it?" Rebecca said, depressed by how difficult it was to track down an arsonist.

"I know it doesn't feel like we're making progress, but we are."

The smile brightening her face had more to do with the "we" part of Zach's sentence than with the "making progress." It was the first time he had openly acknowledged that they were partners.

Zach frowned, knowing precisely what Rebecca was smiling about. The words had just slipped out.

"Don't start getting any cute ideas now," he barked, even though he knew it was too late to take the *we* word back. "I'm putting myself in enough hot water here staying on this case when I've been ordered off. Especially now that I'm officially 'off duty.' If anything happens to you..."

"I know. Fitzgerald and Collins will serve your head on a silver platter," she quipped.

Zach didn't smile. He just kept staring at her. "I want to keep you in one piece." It was the closest he'd come to telling her how he felt about her. Not exactly a profession of love, but his hands were clammy and his stomach was churning. This was as close as he'd come in a long time.

Rebecca gently touched his cheek. "You could use a shave."

He smiled, grateful that she hadn't pressed for any more. "I want to check in with Joe. There should be a report on his desk from the lab."

They went back into the hotel lobby, cut across to the bay of phone booths in a small alcove.

Joe picked up on the first ring. Zach quickly told him about finding Todd.

"That's a big relief," Joe said. "I'll pass it right on to the cops." He hesitated. "Rebecca know?"

Zach's eyes fell on the woman in question. He smiled faintly. "Yeah, she knows."

"Good. That's good." Joe hesitated. "So, you still on vacation?"

"Yeah. I need a wide berth on this one."

"I don't suppose you want any sage advice from me?"

"Save it. I'll need it later."

"I got one good piece of news for you."

"The lab report?" Zach asked.

"You weren't barking up the wrong tree with your nitrite idea. They came up with a definite on amyl nitrite, known in the vernacular as 'poppers.'"

Zach scowled. "Poppers?"

"Sure. You know—kids use 'em in college all the time to stay awake if they're studying for tests, or want to party all night. You snap one in half, take a deep breath, and *boing*—you're wide-awake for hours."

Zach's scowl deepened. "You think our torch is a college kid? Todd thought he was about my age."

Joe laughed dryly. "Could be he's a perennial student."

Rebecca, standing nearby, piped in with another possibility. "Or he lives in a neighborhood close to a college." There were several in Boston to pick from.

"Hey, was that Rebecca I just heard?" Joe asked, amusement heavy in his voice. "So the two of you linked up, huh?"

Linked up was right!

"Do you have anything else for me, Joe?" Zach snapped. How was he supposed to stick to business if everyone around him kept zeroing in on the personal stuff?

"No, that's it for now."

"Okay, I'll be in touch."

"Hold on. Millie called before and wanted to know if Rebecca was coming home for dinner tonight."

Without looking at her, Zach said, "Yes. I'll drop her off by six."

"Drop her off, nothing. Millie's making beef stew. You know you can't resist Millie's beef stew."

There seemed to be a lot of things Zach couldn't resist lately.

"Okay, but I'm taking off early."

Rebecca flashed one of her great grins.

Zach hung up. "What are you so happy about? A man's gotta eat," he muttered.

Before leaving the hotel, Zach placed another call. He wanted to check for messages on his answering machine. There turned out to be one call. He listened to the brief message and hung up.

"Well?" Rebecca prodded.

"It was nothing," Zach said, heading off.

Rebecca hurried after him, catching hold of his sleeve. "Was it from the torch?"

"No."

Rebecca released her hold on him. "I see."

He frowned. "What do you see?"

"It was Eileen, wasn't it?"

He blinked several times. All of a sudden, a woman who could read him like a book. It didn't please him. He kept walking.

Rebecca kept pace with him as they crossed the lobby, neither of them saying anything. He got to the revolving door first, started to step in, stopped and turned to her.

"Yeah. It was Eileen."

Rebecca nodded.

He stepped into one of the pie-shaped glass partitions and pushed. Rebecca slid into the one after him, doing likewise. A cold blast of December air hit them as they stepped out into the street.

Zach pulled up the collar of his brown leather bomber jacket. Rebecca zipped up her parka.

They started down the street for Zach's car. Halfway there, he once again stopped abruptly. "Okay, you want to know why she called? She called because..."

"She had a change of heart," Rebecca finished for him.

"No. She just thought we ought to..."

"Talk?"

Zach reached for a cigarette, then remembered he'd just quit. "Right."

"She didn't think the relationship should end with a recorded message."

Zach stared at her, dumbfounded. "Hell, what are you? A psychic?" Eileen's latest message had made that precise point.

"No, I'm not psychic, Zach. I'm a woman. When she left that first message my bet is she fully expected you to call her back."

"Why would I call her back? She made it clear enough in her message that it was over. I took her at her word. If she was playing games…"

"It's the oldest game there is, Zach. The courting game."

"I'm lousy at games."

"I know," Rebecca said softly, an edge of sadness in her voice. Not that she wanted there to be any game playing between them, but the courting was something else. How she would have loved to be truly courted by Zach.

They went on to his car and got in. Zach pulled out into traffic. He stopped for a red light at the end of the street. He focused hard on the light.

"I'm not calling Eileen back," he said in a low voice. "She had it tagged right the first time. It was never in the cards for us."

Rebecca didn't say anything. He glanced over at her. She was smiling.

10

"ARE WE HAVING FUN YET, Zach, old buddy?"

Zach gripped the receiver tightly. He squinted at his bedside clock. Two-fifteen in the morning. Four days had passed since the fire across the street from his building. Four days since the torch had called him.

"Is this your idea of fun?" Zach asked, reaching for a cigarette. So much for quitting.

"I bet you really think you're something, now. Big hero, movie-star girlfriend. Tell me, Zach. Is she as hot as she looks?"

Zach went cold all over.

"What's the matter, buddy? Cat got your tongue? Or is it Rebecca? Rebecca. Now, that's a real pretty name. Doesn't even begin to do her justice, though, does it?"

All the muscles in Zach's body constricted. "You come within a mile of her and..."

"And what? You'll mow me down with a fire extinguisher? Don't you know yet that you can't put out my fire, Chapin? I'm noncombustible."

"You may think that, pal, but you're on borrowed time. We're closing in."

"Better close in fast then, Zach, old buddy. I think I smell smoke over here on Stuart Street. Hurry if you want to be a big hero again...."

THE FIRE WAS IN A run-down bar and grill on Stuart, right in the heart of the Combat Zone, Boston's tenderloin district where strip joints, porno flicks, and other such sleazy diversions proliferated. When Zach arrived on the scene, the firemen from station house 32 had the fire pretty much under control. Nine people—five male customers, a couple of topless dancers wrapped up in firehouse-issue blankets, the bartender and a muscle-bound bouncer—had made it out without serious injury. The "entertainment" and two of the customers were being treated on the spot for smoke inhalation. The bouncer had a gash in his arm that was being tended to by a paramedic.

Zach was heading over to one of the two fire trucks at the curb to have a word with the fire chief, when the charred sign over the bar and grill caught his eye. He stared at it, a sick feeling rising in his gut. Rebecca's Hot Spot.

"You sure made it here fast, Chapin."

Zach pulled his eyes from the sign and looked over at the young fire lieutenant. "What's the story, Lewis?"

"The bruiser over there said there was this explosion—a bottle of booze blew up and glass went flying a few feet from where he was posted and the next thing he knew the place was ablaze. Sound like arson to you?"

Zach didn't answer. He strolled over to the bouncer whose arm was now wrapped in a bandage. "Bad?" Zach asked.

The bouncer shook his head. "I figure I was lucky."

"You figured right."

"Crazy how it happened. It was like someone threw a bomb into the place. Only I didn't see anyone throw it in."

Zach flipped open a pad and uncapped his pen. "You smell anything funny when the fire started?"

The bouncer, who looked like a pro linebacker who'd seen better days, gave the question careful thought. "Yeah, now that you mention it. There was this...funny smell."

"Kind of like a...popper?"

The bouncer shuffled his feet. "Yeah. Sort of."

Zach felt a hand on his shoulder. It was Joe. Zach had called him as soon as the torch had hung up. Officially, this was his case. And his new partner's. "Where's Adams?"

A smile played on Joe's lips. "Flu. I figured he didn't need to freeze his tootsies off out here in the middle of the night. Told him I'd handle it on my own," Joe said, rubbing his gloved hands together. "Anyone hurt?"

"Nothing serious." Zach hesitated. "Take a look at the sign over the bar."

Joe did, letting out a low whistle. "Glad she didn't hear me sneaking out of the house."

"I don't like it," Zach said. "This torch is one sick cookie. I'm scared he might go after Rebecca. You've got to talk her into getting out of here and going home," Zach said.

"What makes you think she'll listen to me? Besides, Millie's got a houseful coming over Christmas Day to meet her. And don't forget Rebecca's planning to visit that kid, Jerry, in the hospital. You should see the slew of gifts she bought for him and his little brother."

"Right after Christmas Day, then," Zach said resolutely. "If I have to carry her fireman-fashion right onto that plane. It's just getting too damn dangerous."

As Christmas drew close, Rebecca tried her best to get in the holiday spirit. It wasn't easy. After a brief but glorious few moments of being lovers, she and Zach were back to being warriors. He was cool and distant, and adamant about wanting her to leave right after Christmas. Rebecca, however, was set on ringing in the New Year with Zach. If they could track down the arsonist by then, it would be a time to celebrate. And, hopefully, Zach would be in a more conducive mood to deal with personal matters.

On the Saturday night, she and Zach were sitting in a

charming little Italian restaurant in the North End, replete with checkered tablecloths, glowing candles dripping down Chianti bottles and Italian opera lilting out over stereo speakers. She'd invited him to dinner every night that week. He'd made excuses each time until she threatened to do another of her "appearing acts" at his apartment if he turned her down again.

He'd finally accepted her dinner invitation.

"How's your veal scaloppine?" she asked pleasantly.

"Mmm. Great. And your...?"

"Scampi."

"Right. How's your scampi?"

"Terrific."

So much for food talk.

"Zach, I've been thinking...."

He didn't look pleased.

Rebecca didn't let that stop her. "In 'Blue Fire'..."

"Blue Fire?"

"The script about the arsonist."

"Oh, right. The script."

Rebecca snapped a breadstick in half and buttered the tip. "The torch in 'Blue Fire' is this guy who it turns out the heroine Toni Paradisi had actually arrested on arson charges when he was a teenager. He spent a couple of years in jail and when he got out he vowed to show Paradisi that he could take up his trade again, only this time be smart enough not to get caught."

"Let me guess," Zach said dryly. "He gets caught in the end anyway and Toni Paradisi gets a big gold medal pinned on her chest."

Rebecca bit off the tip of the breadstick, and washed it down with a sip of Valpolicella. "What about the torch who did the Drake fire? Is he still in prison?"

Zach shook his head.

Rebecca's pulse quickened. "Well? Wouldn't he be a prime suspect? You got him once. This time he's out to prove he can outsmart you. It would explain why he's calling you, even challenging you. What do you think?"

He smiled crookedly. "I think it would make a pretty obvious movie. I bet the critics would bomb it. No twists, no surprises. Everyone would have it figured out in the first five minutes."

"You're the one that's always saying life's not like the movies. Have you considered him as a suspect?"

Zach shook his head.

"Surely not because it's too obvious," Rebecca persisted.

"Nope."

"Then what? He's got alibis for each fire? He moved away?"

Zach cut off a piece of his veal and popped it into his mouth. "Nope."

She waved the remainder of the breadstick in her hand at him. "So why isn't he a suspect, damn it?"

He dabbed his mouth with his checkered napkin. "He's dead."

Rebecca frowned. "Dead?"

Zach nodded. "Eat your scampi. It's getting cold."

"When did he die?"

He took another bite of veal, then broke off a piece of crisp sourdough bread and began sopping it up with the gravy on his plate. "A few months ago."

Rebecca ignored her scampi, her gaze riveted on Zach. "How did he die?"

Zach bit off a chunk of the gravy-sodden bread. "You don't want to know. It was pretty grim."

"I do want to know," she insisted. "Tell me."

"After dessert. You ever have a cannoli? This restaurant happens to make the finest cannolis in the North End. They don't put the filling in until—"

"Zach," she cut him off, unwilling to drop the subject.

He looked across at her, debating. "He died in a fire," he said finally.

"You mean he went back to his old tricks when he got out of jail?"

"He never got out of jail. He was serving seven-to-ten. He wouldn't have even come up for parole for another two years."

"He died in a fire at the prison?"

There was a short silence before Zach answered. "He set his cell on fire. Lighter fluid."

"Suicide?"

Zach shrugged. "No one knows for sure. He could have been planning a prison break. Or just wanted attention. Or gone bonkers. He wasn't exactly the most stable of characters when he was thrown in the can."

Rebecca scowled. "What about a relative? A father? Mother? Brother? Child?"

"We checked," Zach said. "Hartman was unmarried. No family we could track down. Late fifties. One of your typical loner types."

"Why did he start all those fires?" Rebecca asked.

Zach sighed. "Claimed it was God's will. A master plan to clean up the city."

"Clean up the city? I don't get it."

"He burned down places that a lot of drug users and prostitutes frequented. He was ridding the city of vice." Zach's tone was hard-edged. "Me, I'm partial to rehabilitation programs. Luckily, most of his victims survived."

"Not all of them, though," Rebecca said softly, knowing Zach was thinking about that young girl at the Drake who hadn't been so lucky.

Zach shoved aside his plate. "Come to think of it, the cannolis here have gone downhill. I think we ought to skip dessert. You ready to go?"

Rebecca wanted to tell him he couldn't keep running from his pain, from his feelings, from her. She knew, though, if she said anything, he'd just close himself off even more.

"Why don't we take in a movie?" she suggested, as he motioned to the waiter for a check.

"It's kind of late," he said distractedly. "Aren't the Kellys expecting you back?"

"They didn't give me a curfew," she said dryly.

The waitress brought over the check. Zach pulled a couple of twenties from his billfold before Rebecca managed to get to her wallet.

"I invited you to dinner," she pointed out.

"You can pay next time."

"Will there be a next time?"

Zach was slipping on his coat. "Yeah, sure," he said offhandedly.

They left the restaurant. "How about New Year's Eve?"

Zach was holding open the door for her. "I thought we went over that already, Rebecca. You said you'd leave after Christmas."

They stepped outside. It was snowing hard. "No, you said—"

"You agreed."

"I agreed to think about it."

"So?"

She zipped up her parka. "I thought about it."

"And?"

She didn't answer.

"Don't you ever do anything that makes any sense?" he demanded, his voice edged with frustration.

"I make plenty of sense," she retorted.

"No. You make plenty of dollars, but no damn sense at all."

"Very funny."

"I'm not trying to be amusing."

"You couldn't succeed even if you did try."

They were nose-to-nose, getting blanketed in snow.

"Are you telling me I don't have a sense of humor?" he snapped.

Rebecca put her gloved hands on her hips. "That's precisely what I'm telling you."

"Well, you happen to be dead wrong. I have a perfectly good sense of humor."

Rebecca's eyes narrowed. "Prove it."

Zach's brow arched. "Prove it?"

"That's right. Prove it."

He threw out his hands. "What? Here? Now? What do you want? A stand-up comedy routine out here in the middle of a snowstorm, no less?"

An "I gotcha" smile curved Rebecca's lips. "Told you." She turned away. The next thing she knew she was being pelted by a snowball. She swung around just in time to get another one right in the face.

Zach broke into laughter as the snow ran down her cheeks.

Rebecca glared at him. "You think this is funny?"

He laughed harder.

She pointed to her snow-covered face. "This is not funny, Zach. This just shows what a negligible sense of humor you do have."

"I admit a pie in the face would have been funnier," he said, still laughing. "We could scout around for a bakery. What do you prefer? Chocolate cream or lemon meringue?"

"Ha, ha." She turned in a huff and started down the street.

"Hey, wait!" Zach called out. "Where are you going?"

"To Somerville!" she shouted back.

"The car's the other way."

"I'll take the 'T'."

Zach stared after her. He couldn't believe a couple of snowballs would make her that angry. "Rebecca, don't be like that. Where's your sense of humor? Come on."

She disappeared around the corner.

Zach jogged after her. "Rebecca, come on. I'm sorry, okay?"

She stopped, turning back to him. "It was very juvenile."

He smiled sheepishly as he approached her. "Okay, it was juvenile."

"Very juvenile. Grade-school humor."

His smile deepened. She looked beautiful in the snow. "I guess I have an arrested personality. Let's kiss and make up. What do ya say?"

Rebecca looked at him thoughtfully, like she was debating. Her expression softened. "Okay, Zach." She closed her eyes and slightly puckered her lips.

He smiled, relieved. Then he stepped closer, cupped her face in his hands, bringing his lips to hers. Rebecca stepped in closer, her arms circling his neck. Her lips parted under Zach's....

"Yee—ow!" he shrieked as he felt something very wet and very cold run down his back. A snowball. She'd dropped a snowball under his shirt.

Rebecca broke away, laughing.

Zach was doing a little jig as he pulled his shirttails out of his trousers to shake the snowball out. "This is what you call funny? I'm juvenile? I'm the one with the arrested personality? No sense of humor?" He scowled deeply, then bent down and scooped up a huge handful of snow.

Rebecca started to back away. "Now, Zach. Don't. I was just getting even. We're even now...."

He packed the snow into a ball in his hands.

Rebecca ducked as the ball sailed through the air. When she came up again, she, too, had made a tidy snowball. She got him in the shoulder.

Within seconds, they were making snowballs fast and furiously, flinging them at each other with abandon, both of them laughing hilariously. In a matter of minutes, they were both covered in snow.

"Okay, are we even yet?" she called out, laughing as another snowball got her in the face.

"Nope," Zach said, approaching with his largest snowball to date.

Rebecca began backing off. "What are you going to do with that one?"

He smiled wickedly. "Take a guess."

She backed away some more. "Now, come on, Zach. Enough…is enough."

"Where's your sense of humor, Rebecca?"

She spun around and dashed down the street, laughing. She had a plan. Dash around the next corner, scoop up some snow and as Zach rounded the corner, beat him to the attack.

She could hear Zach laughing as he began chasing her. He was gaining. She picked up speed. Thinking she was home free she ducked around the corner only to skid on the slippery snow and fall right into the arms of a perfect stranger.

"Oh…I'm so sorry," Rebecca gasped breathlessly as she crashed into the man.

The man didn't say anything as she drew back.

Rebecca looked up into the man's face, her expression apologetic. "I really am…sorry."

The man turned his head, his face in shadow, a black wool cap pulled down low. "That's okay," he mumbled, giving a faint nod, and sidestepping her just as Zach was coming around the corner.

Having anticipated a sneak attack from Rebecca, Zach was proceeding with due caution. He was as surprised as Rebecca to find himself nearly colliding with the stranger rounding the corner.

"Sorry," Zach muttered, scooting around him. The man pulled his hat down lower, nodded, and continued on.

Rebecca was standing still, looking after the stranger. Zach didn't notice that she was distracted as he came looming up on her.

"Okay now, you asked for it," he murmured in a mock-menacing voice, a snowball held high in his hand.

Rebecca didn't say a word.

"Come on," Zach taunted good-humoredly. "Aren't you even going to plead for mercy?"

She shifted her gaze to Zach. He immediately saw that something was disturbing her.

"What is it?"

"That guy," Rebecca said.

"What about him? He didn't try anything on you, did he?" Zach looked back over his shoulder, but the man had vanished into the night.

Rebecca shook her head. "No. There was just... something about him."

Zach let the snowball drop from his hand. "What do you mean?"

"It's probably my overactive imagination. It's just that he had a...sort of mean-looking face. I only caught a glimpse of him, really. I suppose there's more than one man with a drawn face and thin lips wandering around Boston. He did give me a start, though."

Zach could see she was shaken. He was sorry now that he hadn't gotten a closer look at the guy. Not that it was particularly likely that they would have run smack-dab into their torch, but Zach didn't doubt the bastard was keeping a close eye on him. And on Rebecca.

He put an arm around her. "This is precisely why I want you to get out of here as soon as possible."

"It's not the only reason, though, is it?"

He drew her to him on the darkened street. The snow was coming down even heavier. A real blizzard. Boston would be having a white Christmas.

He pressed his lips against her snow-wet hair. "I promise you one thing. I'll never forget you. I won't even try."

"You'll probably find another Eileen," she muttered sadly.

He drew her back, cupped her chin. "I'll never find another you, though. You're one of a kind, Rebecca."

"Pushy, stubborn, spoiled..."

He grinned. "Irrepressible, determined, perceptive, and sexy as all get out."

Her hands moved to his face, her brown eyes sparkling. She'd forgotten all about the man who she'd briefly imagined might be their torch. "Is that a round-about proposition, Mr. Chapin?"

His gaze held hers. Zach, too, had forgotten about the man. He had forgotten everything but his charged desire for the woman in his arms. "The roads are pretty bad. Getting you back to Somerville could be a problem."

"A big problem."

He smoothed back her wet hair from her face. "I do want to make love with you, Rebecca. I don't think I've ever wanted anything more."

"Oh, Zach. Neither have I."

Arm in arm, they dashed down the street to Zach's car.

Rebecca was sweeping her parka sleeve across the snow-packed windshield as Zach struggled to turn the key in the lock. The lock had frozen. He tried the other door. No give.

The blizzard was closing in on them. Snow was caking on their hair.

"Now what?" Rebecca asked.

Zach considered for a minute. "We're only a few blocks from the Regis Hotel."

Rebecca brightened. "What are we waiting for?"

Zach caught hold of her gloved hand, holding it

against his chest for a moment. "This doesn't change anything, Rebecca. It's just going to make it harder in the end."

"Nothing's going to make it any harder than it already is," she said softly, brushing her frozen lips against his. "And speaking about being hard..." she murmured, pressing up against him.

Zach laughed hoarsely and they took off at a run for the Regis.

HE HADN'T PLANNED the encounter, had even been distressed by it at first, but now he felt oddly content. He recalled with relish the impact of her body colliding with his, the surprised expression on her face. What surprise there would have been if she had known. But she hadn't. He could see it in the embarrassed, off-handed apology. Although there had been a moment there, before Chapin rounded the corner, when the look she gave him had held a note of curiosity. Had she wondered? What feelings had that stirred in her?

He frowned as he followed them into the lobby of the Regis, ducking behind a pillar as they stepped into the elevator. Revulsion settled over him. He could imagine the two in bed, their naked bodies entwined around each other. Little chance she was thinking about him now; thinking about the power he wielded, the utter destruction he could wreak. All she was thinking about was the hot time she would have with Chapin.

Well, if it was a hot time she wanted...

AS SOON AS they entered the hotel room they came together, busy hands attacking zippers and buttons. Their wet outer clothes fell in a heap on the floor. Quickly, the rest of their clothes joined the pile.

He swept her up in his arms and carried her over to

the bed. Their bodies were cold and they scooted under the fluffy down comforter covering the queen-size bed.

She pressed hard against him, her lips meeting his with fierce impact. Each time they made love there was always a bittersweet intensity at play. Time was the constant. Each time could be the last time. Time was running out. Never enough time. Making each time count. Time had become their enemy.

Zach boldly took possession of every inch of Rebecca's body. Rebecca knew that, at first, she had been as swept up in the danger and excitement as she had been in Zach himself. Now, she knew that it had become more than that. She was truly in love with Zach. And she knew something else, as well: he had spoiled her for all other men.

"Oh, Zach. Zach, you make me feel so good."

He kissed her lips, tasting salty tears. "Don't cry, baby. Please don't cry."

Her chest shuddered as she held back a sob. "I'm not…crying. It's just the…tears."

She rose above him, dipping her head as her lips began to cruise down his chest, the shimmering cascade of her hair fanning out over him like a silk blanket. The tears continued to trickle down her cheeks, falling on his skin, grown warm now. Moist licks of her tongue mingled with the wet tears.

As her mouth seared a path down to his abdomen, Zach's whole body began to tremble. His fingers tangled in her hair as he groaned in anticipation.

Her fingers skimmed lightly along the smooth flesh of his inner thighs as her mouth, too, skimmed smooth flesh. Zach cried out at the indescribably soft eroticism of her caress, the touch so electric he felt devoid of breath.

For an instant, she looked up at him, her luminous brown eyes filled with both love and exquisite desire.

She mouthed the words, "I love you," then dipped her head low, and, lips parted, encircled him.

The wind from the blizzard howling at the windows of their hotel room felt like an extension of their own molten passion. Tears spiked Zach's eyes now as Rebecca took him deep in her mouth. His heart pounded against his chest, reverberating through his whole body.

He drew her up, kissed her hard on the mouth and entered her. Astride him, her head back, lips parted, her voluptuous body undulated in a rhythm all its own. Their cries of pleasure intermingled as they were swept up in an exhilarating helix of texture, scent, sound and motion.

Afterward, Rebecca fell against Zach, sated and exhausted. He wrapped his arms around her, nuzzling his lips against her neck. In the midst of the snowstorm, they both cherished this exquisite moment of pure contentment.

It didn't last long. Within seconds they heard the shrill sound of fire alarms erupting. Rebecca jerked up, panic flashing across her face. Zach was out of bed in an instant. Naked, he rushed to the door. Even before he got there, he saw little curls of smoke drifting under the thin slit between the door and the threshold.

"Quick, get dressed," he ordered, scooping up her clothes and tossing them to her.

They were both dressed in less than a minute. Rebecca ran to the window, hoping to see fire trucks. All she saw were hotel guests and staff streaming out of the hotel in a frenzy of fear.

She spun around to Zach, horror etched in her features. "It was him. I know it was him. He followed us here. He started the fire. I bet he started it right here on this floor." She could feel the hysteria rising in her voice.

Zach could hear it, too. He gave her a sharp look. "We're going to be okay. Just keep your head."

"Keep my head. Right," Rebecca muttered. "That's what I want to do, all right. Keep my head." She forced a smile. "See, I have a sense of humor."

He smiled back. "Good. We'll both need it."

She saw him feel around the door, then reach for the doorknob. "What are you going to do?" she asked, no remnant of humor left in her voice.

"It's close, but I don't think it's too bad yet."

"Zach, the fire trucks should be here any minute. Shouldn't we just wait...?" She was scared. More for him than for her. So this was what love was really all about.

"Stay put. Don't open this door again. I'll come back for you," Zach said.

"Zach..."

He smiled and quickly mouthed some words. It wasn't until after he'd slipped out the door that Rebecca realized he'd mouthed "I love you."

THE INSTANT ZACH STEPPED into the hall, he had to drop down on his stomach because of the smoke. Flames were shooting right under the closed door of the fire exit at the end of the hall, preventing the one emergency route of escape from the building, something several of the hotel guests on the floor had already discovered to their horror.

One patron was about to open the fire door. Zach screamed to him to back away or the whole floor would go. Rising to grab a fire extinguisher off the wall, Zach shouted to everyone to get down, crawl back in their rooms and keep their doors closed. He sounded so authoritative and sure of himself, everyone did as he ordered.

The heat wasn't too bad yet, but the closer he came to the fire exit, the harder it was to breathe. He had his mouth right down on the floor. Despite a bout of coughing, he kept crawling toward the fire, praying that it hadn't spread beyond the capabilities of his trusty fire extinguisher.

REBECCA KEPT STARING OUT the window searching for a sign of the fire trucks. The blizzard had to be slowing them down. Would they get here in time? She'd tried placing a call to Joe Kelly, but the hotel lines were in complete chaos. She stared out the window, wondering if the torch was out there watching, enjoying the destruction he had created. When had he planned this? After bumping into them on the street? She felt certain now, that man she'd run into earlier that evening was the torch. If only she'd gotten a closer look at him. She doubted she could pick him out from a lineup, especially if it was comprised of several stereotypical mean-looking characters. Yet he was unique; a man driven by…what? Revenge? A warped sense of justice? Pure hatred? What was his motive? Why did he want to destroy Zach? And now her?

She placed both palms on the sealed frosted windows, willing the fire trucks to appear. When they did get here would Zach come back into the room and wait with her to be rescued? No. That wasn't Zach's style. He might be an arson investigator now, but he was still a fireman at heart. He would never sit back and wait.

She stared at the closed door. More smoke was seeping underneath into the room. It began to sting her eyes. She wished the window could open so she could take in some gulps of fresh, clean air.

She pounded on the window. Would the firemen even see her when they got here? She was twelve stories up. And the snow was coming down in heavy billows, making visibility negligible. How many, like her and Zach, were still trapped in the hotel?

What was Zach doing out there? Should she obey his

orders and wait in the room for him, or should she go out there and see if she could help him once again? A cat had nine lives. How many did she and Zach have?

FROM BENEATH THE FIRE door oozed heavy black smoke. Zach felt along the door. He guessed that as soon as it opened, it would create a shift in the movement of the air in the hallway, setting up a convection current, so that a tidal wave of flames could come exploding out into the hallway. The flames would billow over him before his fire extinguisher could even make a dent. He would have to come into the fire from above or below the floor he was on. The question was, how to get there?

He raced back down the hallway to the bank of elevators. All of them were jammed. Yanking off the crowbar that had hung beside the fire extinguisher, Zach pried one of the elevator doors open, then held it in place by wedging in a large sand-filled metal cigarette receptacle turned on its side. He looked up and down the dark shaft, spotting the cage several floors below.

Just as he was about to leap out and grab onto the cables, he heard a sharp cry behind him. He spun around.

"Damn it, Rebecca. Didn't I tell you—?"

"This isn't the time to argue with me. What can I do?"

He sucked in a breath and shoved the handle of the crowbar through his belt. "Pray."

Rebecca, far more terrified than she was letting on, nodded.

He winked before he leapt.

Rebecca shut her eyes and prayed.

When she opened her eyes again and looked down the shaft, she saw Zach dangling by his feet from the cable, acrobat-fashion, as he used his crowbar to work at prying open the door of the elevator on the floor below.

Rebecca watched with bated breath.

A creaking noise brought them both up short.

The elevator cage had begun to rise. As if that weren't awful enough, smoke was billowing up from it. Another fire.

Zach could feel the seconds ticking away in his head. Sweat was pouring down his body like a faucet.

He shouted up to Rebecca as he worked. "Get the elevator door closed. If I can get the fire out in the stairwell and it looks safe to make it down that way, I'll open the fire door at the end of the hall and you get everyone out of their rooms."

"I will. I will. Hurry, Zach. Please..."

"If I don't make it within five minutes, get back to your room and wait there."

"You'll make it," she cried, grabbing hold of the metal container keeping the door of the elevator open. She wouldn't pull the obstacle away, though, until she saw Zach get the elevator door below open and get safely inside.

The elevator cage was rising inexorably. Little spurts of flame were shooting out. It was a floor below Zach now. Any second...

Rebecca couldn't breathe. Oh, God, please let him make it.

Her eyes were shut when she heard Zach cry up to her. "Now, Rebecca. Close it now."

She looked down. He'd done it. He'd made it onto the floor below. Tears streaming down her face, Rebecca tugged on the metal container.

Oh, no. It was jammed. She tugged harder. Any second now the cage would reach her floor. Flames would spring out....

She sucked in a deep breath and gathered up all her strength, tugging as hard as she could. It gave, sending her hurtling backward against a hallway credenza.

The doors shut seconds before the flaming cage reached their floor and stopped.

Rebecca stared at the closed doors. She assumed they

were fireproof, but what of the walls above, below, and to the sides? How long would it take before the fire burned through them?

As she hurried down to the fire door, she could hear the sirens in the distance. Minutes later, miraculously, she heard Zach's muted voice from the stairwell. "Okay...Rebecca. Back away...from the...door and get the others," he called out between spurts of coughing.

HE STOOD IN THE CROWD smiling as he watched them come out. He was neither surprised nor disappointed that they'd survived. This fire was but a warning. He was only playing with them. This time.

11

"WOW, REBECCA, THESE games are awesome," Todd exclaimed as he hit the button on the joy stick, an explosion blasting a tank on the television screen. "This is the best Christmas I've ever had in my whole life."

Rebecca tousled Todd's hair—he'd recently gotten a haircut—and smiled at Gail. The sad little boy she'd rescued from the fire had been transformed by this stay with Gail and her parents into a vibrant, engaging child.

"Where are your folks?" Rebecca asked her personal manager.

"Out Christmas shopping, where do you think?" Gail replied with a surreptitious nod in Todd's direction. "Only two shopping days left."

Leaving him to his video games, the two women went into the kitchen, a bright, cheery room with flowered paper, knotty pine cabinets and a large bay window that looked out on Scituate Harbor.

"Coffee?" Gail asked.

Rebecca nodded, leaning against the counter and gazing out the window. The blizzard two nights back had left the boats docked in the harbor under a blanket of snow. Today the sun was shining and Rebecca watched snowflakes melt on the windowsill.

Gail handed Rebecca a mug of coffee. "You want to tell me about your last run-in with the fire department?"

Rebecca was surprised. "How did you hear? Zach

somehow managed to keep our names out of the paper."

"He called me yesterday."

"Zach called you to tell you about the fire?"

Gail nodded. "He's worried sick about you, Rebecca. So am I. So's Sam."

"You didn't phone Sam?"

"Are you kidding? He's still having apoplexy about the last fire you were in. If he heard about this one it would really send him over the edge."

"So why did Zach call you about it?" Rebecca asked warily, guessing what was coming.

"I'm supposed to talk some sense into you." Gail laughed dryly. "I told him I was a manager not a magician."

Rebecca took a sip of coffee. "Did he say anything else?"

Gail cut two slices of the coffee cake her mother had made from scratch that morning. She set one on the counter beside Rebecca. "Not in so many words."

Rebecca set down her coffee mug. "What did he say in not so many words?"

Gail didn't answer right away. She nibbled on her slice of cake. "Rebecca, if you really do care for this guy—" She stopped, shaking her head.

"No, go on. Say it, Gail."

After a moment's deliberation, Gail said quietly, "I know men like Zach Chapin. I grew up with them. Gutsy, rebellious, rough-cut men from working-class families who will dare just about anything, but guard their feelings like Fort Knox. Ordinary Joes. No flash, no glamour, no refined tastes…"

Rebecca folded her arms across her chest. "I know where this is going, Gail. You're trying to tell me that Zach and I are star-crossed lovers. We're from two different worlds. Never the twain shall meet."

"Do you honestly think otherwise?" Gail countered.

Rebecca turned back to the window and stared out at the snowy seascape. "This has nothing to do with how I think. I haven't been able to think straight since I first met Zach." She turned back to Gail, her expression wan. "This is about how I feel. I'm in love with Zach. He's in love with me. All the differences between our life-styles don't add up to a hill of beans as far as I'm concerned."

"You'd better check with Zach's total," Gail said softly. "Even the way the two of you add is different."

Rebecca blinked back tears. "I know. Zach wants me to vanish from his life. He thinks we'll both forget. I won't forget. Neither will he." She managed a weak smile. "I've got one more week to convince him that it's never going to be over between us, whether he likes it or not."

Gail gripped her shoulders. "Zach's scared that it might be over *permanently* if you don't leave right away, Rebecca. You could catch a flight out on Christmas Day. Right after you visit Jerry in the hospital. It leaves at four-fifteen in the afternoon. I could have a limo waiting at the hospital." She hesitated. "I already booked your flight."

"I'm not taking it," Rebecca said stubbornly. "It's too soon. Besides, we're so close to nailing this torch. He's been running the show so far, but now it's Zach's turn. And mine. I've got to be here at the finish if I can, Gail."

"Rebecca, this arsonist is wacko," Gail said, her voice laced with frustration. "You could have died in that fire as easily as escaped. The next time you may not be so lucky."

Rebecca frowned. "Did Zach tell you that I saw him?"

Gail released her. "What?"

"Oh, just a glimpse. It was so damn frustrating. I had this funny feeling when I ran into him—"

"You ran into him?"

"I keep thinking that somehow Hartman is the key."

"Who's Hartman?"

Rebecca stared out the window again. "I cannot shake this feeling that someone out there blames Zach for Hartman's death."

"Hartman died?" Gail shook her head. "What am I saying? I don't even know this Hartman."

Rebecca wasn't listening. She was caught up in her own ruminations. "But who?"

"Who is right," Gail said, her frustration mounting. "What are you talking about, Rebecca? You're not making any sense."

Rebecca grinned at her personal manager. "That's exactly what Zach said to me the other night. It could be, though, that you're both wrong. I may be making perfect sense. Wouldn't that make Zach think twice?"

"Honestly, Rebecca…"

Rebecca gave Gail a little hug. "I've got to go. Merry Christmas and Happy New Year. The same to your folks. I'll just zip into the living room and say goodbye to Todd. It really is terrific of your folks to take him in like this."

Gail smiled. "I have a feeling they might be reluctant to let him go."

Rebecca, who was already halfway out the door, spun back to face her personal manager. "You mean they want to keep him?"

"They're thinking about it. More than thinking, actually. They've talked with Todd's caseworker about becoming foster parents."

"What about Jerry? It would be awful for the two brothers to be split up."

Gail's smile broadened. "They think so, too."

"Oh, Gail, what a Christmas this could turn out to be for those two boys," Rebecca said, tears in her eyes. *What a Christmas this could turn out to be for all of us….*

ZACH CUPPED BOTH HANDS around his glass of club soda while the waitress brought over another beer for Joe.

"Why did she want to know which prison Hartman was sent to?" Zach asked edgily.

Joe shrugged. "Didn't say. Why? Shouldn't I have told her? She could have found out easily enough on her own. All she had to do was check back issues of the *Boston Herald* over at the public library."

Zach ran his fingers through his hair. He needed a haircut, but his mind had been on other things. "I already told her Hartman had no relatives or even any close friends to speak of. No one showed up to give him moral support at his trial. No one cried out in anguish or outrage when he was sentenced."

Joe took a swallow of beer. "Rebecca thinks this case is somehow connected to the Hartman case?"

"That's what she thinks, but she's wrong."

"So, nothing to worry about, then," Joe deadpanned.

Zach scowled. "I'll stop worrying when she boards a plane for L.A. Christmas Day. Her personal manager made all the arrangements."

"Rebecca mentioned at dinner the other night that you two were spending Christmas Eve over at your place."

Zach raised a brow. "That's news to me."

A smile played on Joe's lips. "Maybe it's a surprise."

Another of Rebecca's surprises. That was all Zach needed.

"We'll see you both on Christmas Day, though. I got to tell you, Zach. Millie and the kids are crazy about Rebecca." He hesitated. "They're all kind of..."

"Kind of...what?" Zach asked warily.

"You know. Kind of...rooting for the two of you...to get together."

"Don't be crazy," Zach snapped.

Joe raised his hands in surrender. "Hey, it's not me.

It's Millie and the kids. Is it my fault they all think the two of you make a dynamite match?"

Zach drummed his fingers nervously on his glass. "Dynamite is right.

THE BEACONVILLE Correctional Institution, a maximum-security prison that looked just like the big house where bad guys like Cagney and Bogart had once done movie "time," was located ninety miles north of Boston. When Rebecca drove up to the massive gates, she assumed it might be difficult to get in to see the warden of the prison, but it turned out that Warden Roger Persons was a big fan of hers. The gates opened and one of the guards ushered her right into the warden's office, getting her autograph along the way.

"I've seen all your movies, Miss Fox. Loved every last one of them," Persons, a square-shouldered, square-faced man, exclaimed, shaking her hand and guiding her to a seat. "Oh, there are those who are always complaining that they don't make movies like they used to, but I'm crazy about the movies. Like I said, yours especially."

He shook his head in wonder as he stared at her. "I can't believe that you're even prettier in person than you are on the screen. In fact, I've got to tell you, the camera doesn't do you justice."

"You're too kind, Warden Persons. You really shouldn't flatter me like this."

"Nonsense. You ask the boys around here. They'll all tell you I always tell it like it is." He rubbed his hands together. "Believe it or not, there was a time when I considered giving acting a go. What do you think, Miss Fox?" He flexed impressive biceps. "Would I have had a chance against the Schwarzeneggers and the Chuck Norris types?"

Rebecca flushed. "Well, I…"

"Naw, it wasn't for me. Anyway, I figure it's better to

have something steady and reliable. You know what I mean?''

Rebecca's gaze fell on the barred windows. ''This is certainly steady and reliable, Warden.''

He chuckled. ''Doing time is that, Miss Fox. Whichever side of the bars you're on.''

Rebecca smiled. ''Not everyone has the choice.''

He slapped his knee. ''Good one, Miss Fox. You know, you should do comedy. One of those real old-fashioned slapstick comedies. Something to tickle your funny bone. Bet you'd be terrific.''

''I'd like to do comedy one of these days,'' she said, thinking that a few good laughs *off* the screen would be great, too.

''So, what brings a classy gal like you to a crummy old prison like this, Miss Fox?'' He raised a hand before she could respond. ''No, let me guess. Research for a picture, right? You're doing a prison movie and you want to soak up some of the atmosphere. Am I close?''

''Very close.'' She cleared her throat, eyeing the one wilted fern on the windowsill in the large but barren-looking gray-walled office.

''Actually, I'm going to be doing a film about an arsonist,'' Rebecca said lightly.

The warden nodded thoughtfully. ''Hmm. An arsonist.'' He pointed his index finger at her. ''You won't be playing the arsonist, I hope. I'd hate to see you play a bad guy.''

''Well…no. The arsonist is a man. I happened to be in Boston a few years back and remembered reading about an arsonist who spent some time here.''

The warden's brow furrowed. ''An arsonist that was here? At Beaconville? Well, I suppose we've had our share. Which arsonist was it you were reading about?''

''Douglas Hartman.''

The warden stared at her, saying nothing, his fingers steepled before his face.

"I thought it was a fascinating case."

"Did you, now?"

"He seemed to bear a lot of similarities to the arsonist in the script."

"Really?"

"You see, I'm going to be playing the arsonist's... lover," she lied straight-faced. "And I was wondering if Hartman, by any chance, had a lover," Rebecca went on, edging a little closer to the desk that separated them. "Someone who might have visited him while he was here. Did Hartman have any visitors, Warden?"

The warden seemed to be considering her words carefully. "I'm not really sure. We'd have to check through visitors' books." He paused. "I've got to confess, Miss Fox, that looking into Hartman's time here does make me a little uneasy. You see, we at Beaconville wouldn't want to stir up any old hornets' nests."

"Oh, certainly not," Rebecca said. "I was just thinking that, in order to embrace the character of this woman fully whom I'd be playing in the movie, it would be helpful...."

"I think I see where you're coming from." He puffed out his lips as he gave it some more thought. "Tell you the truth, I find it hard to imagine a man like Hartman having a lover. Cold, distant bastard. Never mixed at all. Never said much. Did hard time until... Well, that's neither here nor there."

"You're right," Rebecca quickly agreed, manufacturing an alluring smile. "Just think, Warden, when you go to see the film you'll have the satisfaction of knowing that you personally helped me get in character."

The warden smiled back. His eyes shifted to the phone. He returned his gaze to Rebecca. "I still can't believe it. Rebecca Fox, right here in my office."

TWENTY MINUTES LATER, Rebecca had a pile of visitors' books in front of her. She opened the first book corresponding with the first month of Hartman's incarceration. She was almost at the end of the second month and was beginning to lose hope that anyone had ever visited him when—bingo—she came upon a name. Janet Chudnow.

Rebecca grew flush with excitement as she saw Janet's name pop up once a month, regular as clockwork, after that. The visits stopped in August. Rebecca guessed that it was in August of last year that Hartman had died in the fire he'd started in his cell.

Rebecca jotted down Hartman's visitor's name, address and phone number. A whirl of questions flooded her mind as she left the prison, the prime ones being, Who was Janet Chudnow and what was her relationship with Douglas Hartman? And with the torch who was after her and Zach?

REBECCA STOPPED at a coffee shop on the tiny main street of Beaconville and put through a call to Zach. He didn't sound exactly thrilled that she'd taken it upon herself to do some sleuthing, but she could detect the hint of excitement in his voice after hearing about the discovery of this mystery visitor. There was even a glimmer of pride in his tone.

Zach told her he'd phone Joe at the bureau and have him bring the Hartman file home with him. They'd all meet at the Kelly house that night and sift through it together on the chance they'd previously overlooked some mention of Janet Chudnow in the notes.

ZACH RUBBED HIS JAW, shaking his head as he poured over the Hartman file that evening after dinner. "Nothing. Not a single mention here of Janet Chudnow."

Rebecca rose from her chair at the Kellys' kitchen table and stood behind Zach, leaning over his shoulder.

"Do you think it was one of those romances that started in prison?"

Zach shrugged. "She could have been one of those do-gooders who visit prisoners who have no family or friends."

Joe brought over some coffee. The house was quiet, as Millie and the two kids were off doing some last-minute Christmas shopping.

Zach got to the end of the file and closed it. Joe looked at the disappointed pair at the kitchen table. "Well, it probably isn't anything anyway. Our torch isn't a woman."

Zach nodded. "And we have no proof this creep we're after is in any way tied in to Hartman."

Rebecca pulled out a small notepad where she'd copied down Janet Chudnow's phone number and address from the visitors' book. Then she walked over to the phone.

"What are you doing?" Zach asked.

"I'm calling Janet Chudnow," Rebecca said blithely.

Zach and Joe shared a look. "Hold it, Rebecca," Zach said. "What are you going to say to her? 'Do you have any connection with the torch that's calling Zach Chapin?'"

Rebecca grinned. "Don't be silly. I'm not going to ask her straight out. I'm just going to find out if she's in. Tell her I'm selling magazine subscriptions."

After two rings, a recording came on the line. "I'm sorry. This number is not in service at this time."

Rebecca hung up, disappointed. "Maybe she stopped paying her phone bills."

Joe cracked a grin. "Spending too much of her dough buying amyl nitrite for her new boyfriend."

Rebecca stared at her notepad. "I think we should take a ride over to 53 Winchester Street and see if she's still living there," Rebecca said. "And maybe talk to some of her neighbors. Find out if any mean-looking characters visit her."

Zach started to try to argue her out of the idea, but Joe seemed to think it made sense.

"Okay," Zach relented, still thinking that the Chudnow connection was a real long shot, anyway. "Here's the deal, Rebecca. I'll let you tag along and help me follow up on this lead if you promise to catch that flight on Christmas Day."

They locked eyes. Joe muttered some excuse and made a hasty exit from the kitchen.

Rebecca waited until Joe was gone. "If that's the way you really want it, Zach."

"It's the way it has to be," he said in a melancholy but resigned voice.

She slipped on her parka. "Okay, let's go."

He caught up with her at the door. "You mean it, now? You'll leave on Christmas Day?"

"Gail will have a limo waiting for me outside the hospital," Rebecca said quietly, facing the door. "Will you come with me to see Jerry?"

He stared at her back. Until she'd come into his life, everything had been going along fine for him. No real highs, but no real lows, either. He flashed on Eileen for the first time in a week. Eileen had been safe. Eileen hadn't gone tearing down walls he didn't want torn down. With Rebecca, it was another story altogether. He was scared that if she didn't get on that plane as planned, the whole kit and caboodle could come toppling down on him.

She turned to face him when she got no answer. "Will you, Zach?"

He'd forgotten the question, but he nodded. There was little he could refuse her, anyway.

A string of triple-deckers lined both sides of Winchester Street, a working-class neighborhood on the edge of Boston's South End. Number 53, like many of its neighbors, was in need of a new coat of paint. Hard, caked snow and ice lined much of the front walk, although a narrow path had been dug out.

There were six mailboxes with buzzers above each lined up to the right of the front door. Several of the boxes didn't have names on them. Chudnow wasn't on any of the ones that did.

Rebecca looked at Zach. Once again she was in her arson-investigator disguise, glasses in place, her hair pulled back, and a wool scarf and hat concealing most of her face. "Which one?"

Zach shrugged. "You pick."

There was no response to the first buzzer she picked. A few moments after trying a second one, an older woman popped her head out of one of the third-story windows. She had a blanket wrapped around her shoulders.

"Who's there?"

Rebecca and Zach stepped back off the porch and looked up at her.

"Sorry to disturb you," Rebecca apologized. "We're trying to locate Janet Chudnow. We weren't sure which apartment is hers."

The gray-haired woman grimaced. "None of them."

"She doesn't live here anymore?" Zach asked.

"She's dead."

The woman started to pull the window back down.

"Wait. How did she die?" Rebecca called out.

"Cops said it was drugs. An overdose." The window started to come down.

"Please, just one more thing," Rebecca pleaded. "Did she live alone? Did she have any family? Anyone who came to visit her? Anyone who…?"

"That's more than one thing," the woman snapped. "And the answer's no. Never saw anyone around. Just as well, too. Probably would have been some of her junkie cohorts."

The window slammed shut. And so did their lead.

12

LIVING ALONE FOR THE past three years, Zach hadn't made much of a fuss on Christmas. The truth was, the holiday depressed him. It was at this time of year more than any other time, that he thought with pangs of longing of how things might have been had he and Cheryl had kids. Not that he ever deluded himself with the fantasy that kids would have held the marriage together, but even if it was in the cards that he would split with his wife, he'd always have had his children. Christmas and kids went together. With kids around, there'd be stockings to hang on his fake fireplace mantel, a Christmas tree to decorate, a wreath to tack up on the door, candles to set aglow in the windows. This was the first Christmas Eve in three years that he hadn't been alone. If memory served him right, he'd celebrated the last two at a solitary table in a local bar.

Rebecca arrived at Zach's place on Christmas Eve laden with gifts and determined to be in good spirits. Not an easy task when her heart was breaking. But then, she was an actress. She laid the brightly gift-wrapped packages on the coffee table and looked around the living room. "Where's the tree?"

Zach gave her a blank look. "The tree?"

"You've got to have a Christmas tree, Zach."

"It would look pretty naked. I don't have a collection of ornaments stored away."

She rezipped her parka and tossed him his jacket. "Come on. We've got to get a tree."

He caught the jacket and stared at her. "Rebecca, it's

Christmas Eve. Where are you going to get a tree? And like I said, I don't have any ornaments."

She grabbed his arm. "So, we'll be creative. We'll string popcorn and make some stuff with origami."

"Ora— What?"

"Japanese paper folding. It's a cinch. We can make birds, boats, stars, anything."

"Christmas isn't exactly a big deal for me, Rebecca," he protested. "Couldn't we just—"

"Oh, Zach, this Christmas is a big deal. For both of us," she said with a bittersweet smile. She crossed to him, standing close enough so that he could smell her orchidy perfume.

He clutched his jacket so he wouldn't pull her into his arms. He'd made a vow before she came that it would be best for both of them if they didn't let things get too "intimate" tonight. Saying goodbye tomorrow was going to be hell enough. He might not get through it in one piece if they ended up in bed tonight. Hell, he wasn't sure he'd get through it in one piece, no matter what.

"Okay, Rebecca. We'll get a tree."

She reached out and touched his cheek, letting her fingers linger for a moment on his rough, familiar skin. "Thanks, Zach."

He felt like crying. So did she.

HE SAW THEM DRAGGING a tree down the street, laughing, joking. They were certainly in the holiday spirit. His tongue snaked out and licked his chapped lips. His hand cupped around his trusty lighter. Back in the trunk of his car were the rest of the fixings he would need to help put him in the holiday spirit, too. He had quite a bagful of festivities planned.

"NO, SILLY. YOU MADE the wrong fold," Rebecca teased, examining the object Zach was holding up for view. "It looks more like a giraffe than a penguin."

He grinned. "So, what's wrong with a giraffe?"

"Absolutely nothing. I've always wanted a giraffe ornament on my Christmas tree." She took it from his hand, poked a piece of string through and hung it on a branch. Then she stepped back and admired the tree, which was festooned with ribbons of popcorn, paper animals and a big aluminum-foil star adorning the top.

"Looking good," Zach said.

Rebecca nodded. "I'll go check on the chestnuts."

Zach caught hold of her as she started for the kitchen. "Wait a sec."

Rebecca's breath held.

He rubbed his thumb lightly across her lips, then released her. "Nothing. I was just wondering when...we were going to open our presents." That was a bald-faced lie. He was wondering about how he was going to make it through the evening without making love with her. *So tell her the truth....*

"I'll get the chestnuts and then we'll open our gifts."

"Great." He couldn't tell her the truth because he knew once he started telling her one truth it would lead to others. Before the night was over, he'd be telling her not to leave. Not tomorrow. Not ever. He looked over at the gifts Rebecca had tucked under their woebegone Christmas tree. All he really wanted for Christmas was...a lifetime of Christmases with Rebecca. Next Christmas, she'd probably be at some glitzy Hollywood party on the arm of a big-time movie star or director, celebrating her star turn in *Blue Fire*. This would all be a faint memory for her. Not for him, though...

Rebecca stood in the middle of the kitchen trying to get back into character. Zach's touch had been electric. She'd almost lost it completely. It was still hard to believe this was it. The end. How was she going to be able to let go? Why did it look so much easier for Zach than it did for her? A part of him would probably be glad to see her go, she decided. She knew she'd turned his life upside down. Well, pretty soon he'd be able to turn it right side up again.

A minute later she popped back into the living room with a plateful of piping-hot chestnuts. "They smell wonderful even if we didn't roast them on an open fire," she said with sitcom enthusiasm.

They sat together on the floor by the tree. "Open mine first," she said, handing him a large box.

"What did you do?" he asked, looking at the large stack. "Buy all the stores out?"

"Not all of them."

He began unwrapping the paper. "I'm not much of a shopper. I feel bad. I didn't get you a pile of gifts."

"I love shopping. It's one of the things I do best."

He opened the box. Inside was an exquisite maroon silk robe. "Wow."

"I was going to get it monogrammed, but then I decided you really weren't the monogram type."

He smiled. He didn't have the heart to tell her he wasn't the silk-robe type, either. "It's great, Rebecca. Thanks."

She gave him another box. Inside was a pair of sheepskin-lined leather gloves. "Your hands are always cold," she said. *Not your heart, though. You've got a warm heart, Zach.*

He kept opening boxes—a chamois shirt, a brown leather vest, a cashmere scarf. "When do you open your gift from me?"

"After this last gift," she said, handing him one final box.

He opened it slowly. Inside, was a book. *I Love Los Angeles: A Tour Guide for the New Resident.* He stared at the book, then looked at her.

"Life's unpredictable," she said softly. "You never know."

He started to speak. She put her finger to his lips. "Don't say anything, Zach." She gave him a sad smile.

He reached into his trousers pocket and pulled out a small box, handing it to her in silence.

She studied the tinfoil-covered package for a moment. "You wrapped it yourself."

"I'm not much of a wrapper, either," he said, smiling crookedly.

She kept staring at it.

"Go on. Open it," he prodded.

She felt a tremor go through her as she painstakingly undid the wrapping. It might have been gold leaf rather than tinfoil. The box was velvet, a bit larger and flatter than one that would hold an engagement ring. She could feel Zach's eyes on her as she slowly lifted the lid.

Her eyes widened.

"What do you think?" Zach asked anxiously.

She gently plucked out the shiny gold star. Rebecca's name was engraved on the top. In the center were inscribed the words, *For Exemplary Service*.

Zach took it from her hand and tenderly pinned it on her sweater.

Tears rolled down Rebecca's cheeks. She opened her mouth to say something, but no words came out.

"Don't," he murmured softly.

She placed her hand over the medal that he'd pinned close to her heart. Then she sagged against him, crying into his sweatshirt.

He put his arms around her. A comforting gesture. But there was no comfort to be had. For either of them. There was only want. And need.

"Oh, Zach…"

He drew her down on the rug right in front of their ragtag Christmas tree, slowly, gently undressing her. As soon as he stripped out of his clothes, he enfolded her against him.

She trembled, sighed with relief. Then she raised her head, cupping his face and kissed him deeply. A long, frenzied kiss. Zach's hands stroked her thighs, her stomach, her breasts.

She reached down between them, took him in her hand, held him, felt his life force pulsating in her grasp.

He rolled her onto her back. She pulled him on top of her, gripping him with her fine, slender thighs as she guided him into her. She pulled her legs higher and higher, hips arching, wanting more than union. Wanting. Wanting...

It was like walking into a fire—fierce, dangerous, terribly exciting, separate from the real world; apart; beyond.

The startling ring of the phone jarred them back to reality. They stared at each other, neither of them saying a word, both of them thinking the same thing.

He rolled off her. Rebecca started to beg him not to answer the phone, but she knew he had to.

He picked up on the fourth ring. He didn't say a word. He just listened, the tender, loving expression on his face hardening into granite. He hung up, not turning back to her.

"Another fire."

Rebecca sat up, started reaching for her clothes. When she picked up her sweater her eyes lingered for a moment on her bright, shiny Christmas gift. She gently ran her fingertips over it before she slipped the sweater on.

Zach dressed quickly, then put in a call to the fire station and to Joe. When he finished his last call, he turned to Rebecca who was now fully dressed and sitting almost primly on the sofa.

"I don't want you down there," he said quietly but firmly. One more day and she'd be safely away. He didn't want to take any chances. If anything happened to her...

Rebecca knew what was going through his mind. "Okay, Zach."

He managed a weak smile. "I'll call you as soon as things are under control."

She nodded. He slipped on his coat and started for the door. She caught up with him as his hand was gripping the doorknob, and threw her arms around him.

He gave her a quick kiss on the forehead, knowing if he did anything more he might not be able to concentrate on tackling the mess facing him.

He was down the hall when she called out, "Be careful."

He gave her a thumbs-up sign as he stepped into the elevator. She returned the gesture.

LEFT ALONE IN ZACH'S apartment, Rebecca felt edgy and helpless. This was just the kind of "role" she didn't want to play. There had to something she could do. And then an idea struck her. She hurried into the kitchen on a hunt for Zach's phone book. She found it tucked in a cupboard.

She began riffling through the pages until she got to the C's. Why hadn't she thought of it earlier?

Cha—Chi—Chu—

It was a long shot, but there was just a chance....

There it was. Chudnow. Not one, but two. Philip Chudnow in Dorchester and Rory Chudnow in Boston proper. She dialed the first. A woman answered.

"Could I please speak to Philip Chudnow?" Rebecca asked politely. Once she heard his voice on the phone, she'd know.

"I'm sorry. Phil isn't here."

No doubt he was out watching another building go up in smoke.

"When do you expect him in?"

There was a pause. "I don't."

"You don't expect him back?"

"Not for another couple of months. He's on an oil rig in the middle of the Atlantic. Been there for over a month. What did you want to speak to him about?"

"Oh...I was just wondering if he was interested in a magazine subscription," Rebecca said lamely, already tapping Rory Chudnow's phone number.

"We have all the magazine subscriptions we need." Click.

Rebecca quickly dialed again, praying for better luck this time. She let the phone ring a dozen times. No answer. No answering machine. Rebecca copied down the address. It sounded familiar. Stuart Street. Stuart Street?

A chill rippled down her back. She remembered. A bar had been burned down by the torch on Stuart Street. Joe had snuck out on her the night of the fire so she hadn't seen it herself, but that next morning she'd overheard him telling Millie the fire had been in a bar on Stuart Street in the Combat Zone. Right in Rory Chudnow's neighborhood. How convenient.

Rebecca felt a rush of excitement. Call it instinct, woman's intuition, anything. She knew. The man they were after was Rory Chudnow. All the pieces fit. Or, at least, most of them.

Scribbling a note to Zach as to where she was going, Rebecca hurried out of the apartment. She was going to pay a visit to Rory Chudnow's address. While he was off playing with matches, she might be able to get into his place and find some evidence that would nail him for Zach.

HE WAS ADEPT AT breaking into buildings, getting past locked doors. Zach Chapin's apartment was no exception. He stepped silently inside, his plan being to surprise Rebecca. A real fiery surprise. He'd seen Chapin take off without her a minute after he'd called. As soon as he saw the old Ford pull out, he ducked into the alley and began working on the locked basement door. It had taken him a few more minutes than usual because the lock had frozen.

He sneered at the stupid-looking Christmas tree and all the opened gifts strewn on the floor in the empty living room. He peered cautiously in the kitchen. Empty, too. Stealthily, he crossed to the bedroom, expecting to find her tucked in bed, waiting for her hero to return. Little did she know that when her hero did return, he'd be in for a big surprise. How would Chapin take it? Losing someone he loved? Would it break Chapin's heart in two as it had his when he lost the one person he most loved? An eye for an eye, the Bible said.

A cold fury enveloped him when he saw that the bedroom was empty. She was gone. He had it all planned, but she was gone. Like a man possessed, he searched the small apartment again. Empty. She must have slipped out the front of the building while he was struggling with the basement door in the alley. He stormed back into the living room. Then he saw the note on the coffee table.

His eyes narrowed as he read it. Then a diabolical smile lit his face. He crumpled the note, then set it afire with his lighter.

The phone rang. Two rings and the machine clicked on. Chapin's recorded voice. A beep. Then Chapin's voice in the flesh. A very anxious voice.

"Rebecca? Are you there? Rebecca, pick up, damn it. Listen, the fire was a false alarm."

He laughed diabolically. "This one isn't," he said in a voice of heightened excitement. "This one's for real."

"Rebecca, where the hell are you? Listen, I'm coming right back home." Click.

"You're gonna be too late," he said as he snapped a popper in half, took a deep sniff, then lit it with his lighter....

BY THE TIME ZACH AND Joe made it across town, firemen were coming out of his building. Zach could feel the bile rise in his throat. His whole body broke into a sweat.

Joe stopped to talk to one of the firemen. Zach was already racing up the stairs. Joe caught up with him, huffing and puffing.

"They say no one was in there, but the apartment is pretty well gutted," Joe said, trying to catch his breath.

"Then where the hell did she go?" Zach fought against letting his worst fear surface, but it was impossible to hold it back. What if the torch had kidnapped Rebecca?

RORY CHUDNOW LIVED IN a tenement, the first floor of which was occupied by a strip joint. Rebecca had second thoughts as she stared up at the building. Maybe she should have waited for Zach. She considered calling Fitzgerald, but he'd probably blame Zach for letting her continue working on the torch case. Besides, what if her instincts were wrong? What if this Rory Chudnow was no relation to Janet Chudnow? What if he wasn't the torch? She needed to get her hands on some concrete evidence. The only way she was going to get it was to go have a look inside his apartment.

She dialed Chudnow's number once again from a bar across the street. Still no answer. The coast was clear. The question was, for how long?

ZACH STORMED INTO HIS ravaged, smoke-laden apartment, Joe right behind him. The Christmas tree was a heap of charred ash. All the lovely gifts Rebecca had given him had also gone up in smoke. He was glad, at least, that he'd pinned that medal to her sweater. It would have broken her heart if it had burned, too. If her heart wasn't broken already. If she was still alive. He closed his eyes and swayed a little, having to grip the back of a chair for support. He took a steadying breath and walked aimlessly into the devastated kitchen.

Joe went to the phone in the living room, but it was unusable. "I'll go next door and call home. Maybe she went back there," he called out to Zach.

"No. Wait!" Zach shouted back.

Joe hurried into the kitchen. Zach was staring down at a charred open phone book. He could just make out a couple of names. They began with the letter C.

Joe got hold of a neighbor's phone book. Minutes later, after first trying Philip Chudnow and having a brief conversation with his wife, they were racing in Zach's car for Rory Chudnow's apartment in the Combat Zone.

ONCE, IN A MOVIE, Rebecca had used a credit card to get into an apartment. She decided to give it a try on Chudnow's door and was tickled pink when the lock gave way.

The adrenaline was flowing when she creaked open the door. The place was a dive. Two claustrophobic rooms decorated sparsely with Salvation Army rejects. After a quick check of the living room, Rebecca stepped into the tiny, airless bedroom. There was a narrow wooden-framed unmade bed, a bureau, and a closet. Nothing else.

Rebecca spotted the framed photo on the bureau. It was a portrait of a middle-aged woman. Drawn face, weary eyes, a pained smile. It was signed. To Rory. All My Love, Mom.

Rebecca would have bet anything "Mom" was Janet Chudnow. She set the photo down and went over to the closet. Rory Chudnow was definitely no clotheshorse. There was one frayed sport jacket, a couple of shirts, a pair of gray slacks, a pair of worn jeans. And a lined raincoat. Rebecca pulled the raincoat out and stared at it, wide-eyed.

One gold button was missing from the coat. The others were a perfect match to the one she'd found in the fire across from Zach's building. Her heart started to race, her pulse beating in her ear. She tossed the coat over her arm. A real honest-to-goodness piece of evidence. Wasn't Zach going to be proud of her?

On the shelf above the closet was a carton. Rebecca reached up for it and set it down on the floor. Kneeling, she opened it. Her breath held. Inside the carton were stacks of vials of amyl nitrite. Poppers!

Just as she was extracting one of the vials, a hand clamped down over her mouth. Stunned, Rebecca froze. She hadn't heard anyone creep into the room, but she didn't need three guesses to know who it had to be.

"Justice at last," a voice murmured huskily in her ear.

Rebecca's heart started pounding so hard, she thought it would erupt right through her chest.

"An eye for an eye." He spoke louder as he pulled her to her feet, one hand still clamped over her mouth, the other locked around her waist.

She recognized his voice now—the same ominous baritone as the voice on the phone. She began struggling, but his grip on her merely tightened. He dragged her over to the bed and threw her down on it.

That was when she saw him for the first time.

No, it was the second time. She could see now, without a doubt, that Rory Chudnow had been the man she'd bumped into on the street that other night. She stared at him with terrified eyes.

"Don't move or I'll hurt you. You don't want me to hurt you. But I will if you cross me. And I'll enjoy it."

He loomed over her. She was terrified that he'd rape her, torture her. She didn't move a muscle. "Why?" Her voice was a bare croak.

"You want to know why? I'll tell you. Chapin destroyed everyone I cared about. Doug Hartman was my uncle, my mother's stepbrother. She didn't even know he'd been thrown into jail until she moved to Boston a couple of years ago."

He leaned down closer. Rebecca could smell alcohol on his breath. And something else. Venom. "I was living in Chicago when he died. Mom wrote me, told me all about how it was Chapin's fault. He'd put her brother in prison when all he was trying to do was rid this country of scum. My mother hated Chapin. So did I." His eyes grew distant. He was somewhere else. Locked in an ocean of hatred.

"My mom killed herself in grief...."

"She died of a drug overdose," Rebecca said. "It could have been an...accident."

"Shut up." He slapped her hard across the face.

Tears welled in her eyes, but she wouldn't give the bastard the satisfaction of crying out in pain or fear.

"I came to Boston. I vowed I'd get him. First I'd make him a laughingstock. Then... Then I'd watch him burn. Just like poor Uncle Doug burned. I wouldn't be surprised if Chapin was behind that fire."

He smiled down at her. "I had it all neatly planned. Then you walked yourself right into my little lair. Now, I've got a better plan. I'll kill you first and leave Chapin alive for a while. Just long enough to suffer real good. Like I've been suffering. Then I'll give him a break." He smiled broadly. "I'll put him out of his misery."

Rebecca looked into Rory's intense, excited, crazy eyes. If he were an actor playing the part of the arsonist in "Blue Fire," the director might have gotten on his case for overacting. This wasn't a movie, though. This was real life. And Rory wasn't acting at all. Rebecca could see that the man was totally unhinged.

She cringed in revulsion as he stroked her cheek. He seemed oblivious to her response. "Too bad we don't have more time. I could show you what a real man is like."

Rebecca squeezed her eyes shut. *Oh, Zach, I'm sorry I didn't stay put. I love you, Zach. Please forgive me....*

He began tying her to the bed. She struggled, but he was far too strong for her.

"You're wrong about Zach," she told him. "He's not going to grieve over my death. He doesn't love me. I'm leaving tomorrow. It was his idea. He grew bored with me. It's over...."

"I'd never grow bored with you, beautiful." He finished the task. "Pity your time is up."

"No. Please—"

The rest of her words were cut off as a wad of cloth was stuffed into her mouth and then a strip of masking tape stuck across it.

Rebecca watched in horror as he snapped a popper in half, inhaled deeply, then used it to start a fire in one corner of the tiny bedroom. Once it took, he rose and looked over at her with a demented smile. "It won't be long now," he said, then blew her a kiss and left the apartment.

ZACH BURST INTO THE tenement just as Rory Chudnow got to the bottom landing. He saw the look of panic flash across Rory's face as he started to race by him.

Zach grabbed him and threw him up against the wall. "It's over, Chudnow."

Chudnow suddenly smiled. "Almost."

That was when Zach smelled the smoke. Chudnow broke free and slammed a fist hard into Zach's jaw, sending him sprawling sideways. Then he spun around and flew to the door, only to spot Joe a few feet away. No place to go but up. He headed up the stairs.

Joe helped Zach struggle to his feet. Once he was upright, Zach took off after Chudnow, two steps at a time. Joe followed.

Zach caught up with Chudnow on the third floor. Smoke was drifting out from under one of the doors. Shoving Chudnow aside, he raced for the door, kicking it open. Chudnow leaped at him, pummeling him. Zach spun around and caught Chudnow with a hard chop to the neck. Chudnow fell backward, practically landing right in Joe's arms.

THE EDGE OF THE SHEET had started to burn as Rebecca lay there tied to the bed, helpless, terrified, praying that somehow Zach would arrive in time to rescue her. But that was only in the movies. This was real life. The heroine didn't get saved at the last minute in real life.

Then, suddenly, there he was. Tearing at the bindings, ripping the tape off her mouth. She spit out the rag as he gathered her in his arms. In the distance she could hear sirens ringing.

"Oh, Zach, what a finale," she gasped, throwing her arms around his neck as he carried her to safety.

ON CHRISTMAS DAY, Rebecca and Zach visited Jerry in the hospital. Millie, Joe and the kids came along. So did Todd, Gail and her parents. The McCarthys had brought good news. The court had made them foster parents for both Todd and Jerry. Jerry had some terrific news of his own. He was getting out of the hospital in another week.

Jerry was just finishing opening all his gifts—he was totally speechless when he unwrapped the portable CD player and the pile of rap CDs from Rebecca—when new visitors arrived.

Rebecca was startled to see the fire commissioner and the fire marshal enter the room.

Fitzgerald and Collins nodded to Zach, Joe and the others, then focused their attention on Rebecca.

"We knew you were leaving today," Fitzgerald said

to her, looking very formal in his brass-buttoned blazer, striped tie and white shirt, "so we've come down here, Rebecca, to present you with a special commendation on behalf of the city of Boston and the Bureau of Arson Investigation, for being instrumental in bringing an arsonist to justice."

Collins, dressed in his braided uniform, gave her a little salute, then opened a velvet box inside of which was a gold star. Her name was engraved on it. Beneath her name were the words, *For Exemplary Service*.

Fitzgerald pinned it right next to the gold star she was already wearing on her sweater. Everyone in the room applauded. Rebecca's hand cupped both medals, her gaze falling on Zach. "I'd rather have these than an Academy Award." Her voice cracked and she had to fight back the tears.

He came over and put his arm around her. "If I know you, you'll get one of those, too. And you'll deserve it."

A nurse popped into the room. "Miss Fox? You're limo is waiting."

Rebecca nodded. Now that the torch had been captured, both she and Zach knew it would have been physically safe for her to stay until New Year's Day, but they also knew it wouldn't be emotionally safe for either of them. If it was going to end—and it was—better not to drag out the pain of parting. A clean break. Ha!

Rebecca kissed everyone in the room while Zach stood waiting for her in the hall. Millie hugged her tightly. "We'll keep in touch. And don't worry. We'll work on him."

Gail squeezed her hand. "See you back in La La Land on the second."

THEY RODE DOWN THE elevator, not touching, not speaking. When they entered the lobby, Rebecca stopped abruptly and unbuttoned her coat. For a moment Zach thought she'd decided not to go. He knew if she backed out now, he wouldn't protest. Protest nothing. He'd pull her into his arms and he'd never let her go. To hell with what made sense.

Then he saw that she was removing the gold star that she'd just been awarded. "What are you doing?" he asked.

She pinned it to the collar of his jacket. "I'll wear yours and…you wear mine. It's a link, Zach. It's a link."

He pulled her into his arms and kissed her deeply, both of them oblivious to the curious stares of the people in the lobby.

"I love you, Zach."

"I love you, Rebecca."

They walked out to the limo. He helped her in. She smiled wanly at him, touching his cheek one last time. "Fade out. The end."

Tears were running down his cheeks as he watched the limo drive off. She was wrong. It would never end.

Epilogue

THE ROOM WAS DIM, jazz playing quietly in the background. They were all alone. Her back was to him.

"We've got to end it. This is crazy," she said, her voice a pained whisper.

"*Crazy's* the word," he said huskily, spinning her around, pulling her into his arms. "I'm crazy about you. You're crazy about me."

She drew back, smoothing her tangled hair from her face. "What about our crazy arsonist?"

He cupped her face. His hands were trembling slightly. "He's not ours. He's mine."

She shook herself free of his touch. "Don't fight me on this one. I was at that fire. It was awful. I've never seen anything like it. There must have been a hundred people—" Her voice cracked. She couldn't go on.

"Baby," he murmured, drawing her against him. "It's okay."

"No, it isn't okay. Nothing's okay," she said with anguish. "Oh, Will, I'm scared."

"Don't be scared, Toni. I'm never going to—"

"Cut," a voice boomed, Eliot Mason climbing down from his director's perch beside the cameraman. He approached Steve Shields who was playing William Bower and gave him a little nod. Then he put his arm around Rebecca.

"That was terrific, honey. The thing is, there was a little too much intensity. This is only our first day. I'm afraid you're going to burn out before we get to the end of this shoot. Sure, Toni's scared at this point. But she's also a tough cookie. She knows she can hack it, with or without him." He smiled at her. "Right?"

Rebecca forced a faint smile. "Right." The problem was, this film was so close to home. Toni Paradisi might be able to hack it with or without William Bower, but she wasn't so sure she, Rebecca Fox, could hack it without Zach Chapin.

Mason gave her a little squeeze. "You're a natural for this part, Rebecca. I've got to tell you, any doubts I may have had... Well, all I can say is those weeks in Boston were well spent."

"They were that," Rebecca murmured. "The best weeks of my life."

"You've added a whole new dimension to your acting," Mason said enthusiastically. "This part could be your ticket to the Academy Awards."

Tears welled in Rebecca's eyes, her hand slipped inside her suit jacket to her shirt where she'd pinned Zach's gold star right over her heart. It still meant more to her—and always would—than any trophy for acting. She thought about her gold star. Was Zach still wearing it? Did he miss her as much as she missed him? Was he as lonely, depressed? Did he toss and turn at night in his bed? Three weeks and not one word from him. Not even a postcard. A nice, clean break. Only there was nothing nice and clean about it. It hurt like hell.

"Why don't you take a fifteen-minute break?" Mason suggested. "Go back to your trailer, have a nice tall glass of iced tea..."

Rebecca nodded. She did need a little time to pull herself together before another take. Fifteen minutes to learn how to "act" as if she could hack the ordeal ahead of her.

WHEN SHE WAS HEADING back to the set, she spotted Mason off in a corner having a powwow with another man. The man's back was to her and the light was dim, but something about him reminded her of Zach. This wasn't the first time. For the past three weeks, she'd spotted a dozen men that, from a distance, she thought might be Zach. They never were.

She told herself she had to stop this. Pretty soon she'd start having delusions. Mason turned, spotted her, waved and started toward her. The man he'd been talking to walked off. Rebecca watched him head for the exit.

He walked with a slight limp.

Rebecca's heart stopped.

Mason came up to her. "We'll be ready for your scene in about ten minutes. How's—"

She grabbed his sleeve. "Who was that man you were talking to?"

"The man? Oh, that's the guy I hired as an arson consultant for the film."

Rebecca stared at Mason. "An…arson consultant?"

The portly director cracked a smile. "I think you already know him. The name's Chapin."

She was already running across the set before he finished.

She stopped just outside the soundstage. He still had his back to her. He was smoking a cigarette.

"I thought you quit," she called out, her voice tremulous.

He turned slowly. Something glinted on his shirt. Her gold star.

"I couldn't. I tried." He flicked the cigarette and started toward her. "But I couldn't."

"Smoking's dangerous for your health."

"Smoking? Oh, that was my last cigarette." He stared at her, drinking her in, knowing now that he would never get enough of her. "I was talking about you, sweetheart," he said with a roguish smile. Then his expression turned serious. "I couldn't quit thinking about you, Rebecca. Wanting you. Missing you. Needing you."

She flew into his arms, feeling alive for the first time in weeks.

"Oh, Zach, what happens when the movie's...over?"

He held her tight, the circle complete. "I've been offered the job of fire marshal for the L.A. Bureau of Arson Investigation. Time to settle down." From his back pocket, he withdrew a copy of the guidebook she'd given him, the original having burned in the fire at his apartment on Christmas Eve. "Not a bad city. I think I could get used to it."

"It's a great city," she murmured, tears spilling from her eyes. "Now."

He stroked her fine auburn hair that glistened in the California sunshine. "Marry me, Rebecca. Together we'll set the world on fire."

"No. No more fires, Zach. Together we'll make some beautiful babies. And if we're lucky, when next Christmas rolls around we'll be hanging three stockings on our mantel, and we'll decorate our Christmas tree with..."

"Paper giraffes?"

"Absolutely."

He pulled her back into his arms and they kissed deeply. Then he drew her gently from him and pinned her hard-won gold star on her chest. Right next to his. "For exemplary service, Rebecca Fox. Above and beyond...my wildest dreams."

She put her hand over her heart. "Now this is what I call a perfect Hollywood ending."

FADE OUT...

American HEROES
AGAINST ALL ODDS

1. ALABAMA		**26. MONTANA**	
After Hours—Gina Wilkins		*Angel*—Ruth Langan	
2. ALASKA		**27. NEBRASKA**	
The Bride Came C.O.D.—Barbara Bretton		*Return to Raindance*—Phyllis Halldorson	
3. ARIZONA		**28. NEVADA**	
Stolen Memories—Kelsey Roberts		*Baby by Chance*—Elda Minger	
4. ARKANSAS		**29. NEW HAMPSHIRE**	
Hillbilly Heart—Stella Bagwell		*Sara's Father*—Jennifer Mikels	
5. CALIFORNIA		**30. NEW JERSEY**	
Stevie's Chase—Justine Davis		*Tara's Child*—Susan Kearney	
6. COLORADO		**31. NEW MEXICO**	
Walk Away, Joe—Pamela Toth		*Black Mesa*—Aimée Thurlo	
7. CONNECTICUT		**32. NEW YORK**	
Honeymoon for Hire—Cathy Gillen Thacker		*Winter Beach*—Terese Ramin	
8. DELAWARE		**33. NORTH CAROLINA**	
Death Spiral—Patricia Rosemoor		*Pride and Promises*—BJ James	
9. FLORIDA		**34. NORTH DAKOTA**	
Cry Uncle—Judith Arnold		*To Each His Own*—Kathleen Eagle	
10. GEORGIA		**35. OHIO**	
Safe Haven—Marilyn Pappano		*Courting Valerie*—Linda Markowiak	
11. HAWAII		**36. OKLAHOMA**	
Marriage Incorporated—Debbi Rawlins		*Nanny Angel*—Karen Toller Whittenburg	
12. IDAHO		**37. OREGON**	
Plain Jane's Man—Kristine Rolofson		*Firebrand*—Paula Detmer Riggs	
13. ILLINOIS		**38. PENNSYLVANIA**	
Safety of His Arms—Vivian Leiber		*McLain's Law*—Kylie Brant	
14. INDIANA		**39. RHODE ISLAND**	
A Fine Spring Rain—Celeste Hamilton		*Does Anybody Know Who Allison Is?*—Tracy Sinclair	
15. IOWA		**40. SOUTH CAROLINA**	
Exclusively Yours—Leigh Michaels		*Just Deserts*—Dixie Browning	
16. KANSAS		**41. SOUTH DAKOTA**	
The Doubletree—Victoria Pade		*Brave Heart*—Lindsay McKenna	
17. KENTUCKY		**42. TENNESSEE**	
Run for the Roses—Peggy Moreland		*Out of Danger*—Beverly Barton	
18. LOUISIANA		**43. TEXAS**	
Rambler's Rest—Bay Matthews		*Major Attraction*—Roz Denny Fox	
19. MAINE		**44. UTAH**	
Whispers in the Wood—Helen R. Myers		*Feathers in the Wind*—Pamela Browning	
20. MARYLAND		**45. VERMONT**	
Chance at a Lifetime—Anne Marie Winston		*Twilight Magic*—Saranne Dawson	
21. MASSACHUSETTS		**46. VIRGINIA**	
Body Heat—Elise Title		*No More Secrets*—Linda Randall Wisdom	
22. MICHIGAN		**47. WASHINGTON**	
Devil's Night—Jennifer Greene		*The Return of Caine O'Halloran*—JoAnn Ross	
23. MINNESOTA		**48. WEST VIRGINIA**	
Man from the North Country—Laurie Paige		*Cara's Beloved*—Laurie Paige	
24. MISSISSIPPI		**49. WISCONSIN**	
Miss Charlotte Surrenders—Cathy Gillen Thacker		*Hoops*—Patricia McLinn	
25. MISSOURI		**50. WYOMING**	
One of the Good Guys—Carla Cassidy		*Black Creek Ranch*—Jackie Merritt	

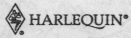 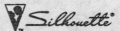

Please address questions and book requests to: Harlequin Reader Service U.S.: 3010 Walden Ave., P.O. Box 1325, Buffalo, NY 14269 CAN.: P.O. Box 609, Fort Erie, Ont. L2A 5X3   PAHGEN

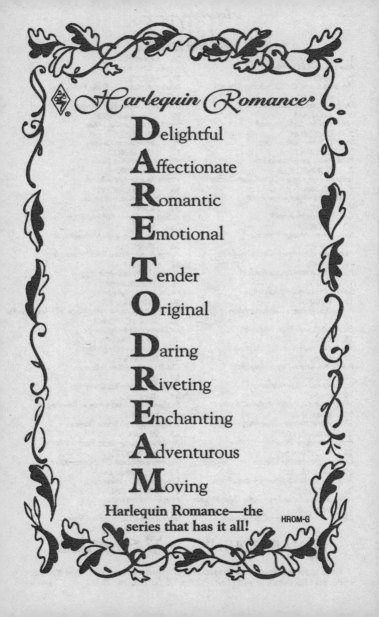

Harlequin Romance®

Delightful

Affectionate

Romantic

Emotional

Tender

Original

Daring

Riveting

Enchanting

Adventurous

Moving

Harlequin Romance—the
series that has it all!

HROM-G

HARLEQUIN PRESENTS®

**The world's bestselling romance series...
The series that brings you your favorite authors,
month after month:**

Helen Bianchin...Emma Darcy
Lynne Graham...Penny Jordan
Miranda Lee...Sandra Morton
Anne Mather...Carole Mortimer
Susan Napier...Michelle Reid

and many more uniquely talented authors!

Wealthy, powerful, gorgeous men...
Women who have feelings just like your own...
The stories you love, set in exotic, glamorous locations...

HARLEQUIN PRESENTS,
Seduction and passion guaranteed!

Visit us at www.eHarlequin.com   HPGEN00

Harlequin® Historical

From rugged lawmen and
valiant knights to defiant heiresses
and spirited frontierswomen,
Harlequin Historicals will
capture your imagination with
their dramatic scope, passion
and adventure.

Harlequin Historicals…
they're too good to miss!

HHGENR

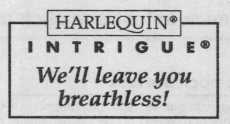

HARLEQUIN®
I N T R I G U E®
We'll leave you breathless!

If you've been looking for thrilling tales of
contemporary passion and sensuous love stories
with taut, edge-of-the-seat suspense—
then you'll *love* **Harlequin Intrigue!**

Every month, you'll meet four new heroes
who are guaranteed to make your spine tingle
and your pulse pound. With them you'll enter
into the exciting world of Harlequin Intrigue—
where your life is on the line
and so is your heart!

THAT'S INTRIGUE—DYNAMIC ROMANCE AT ITS BEST!

 HARLEQUIN®
I N T R I G U E®

INT-GENR

Romance is just one click away!

online book **serials**

➤ *Exclusive* to our web site, get caught up in both the daily and weekly online installments of new romance stories.

➤ Try the Writing Round Robin. Contribute a chapter to a story created by our members. Plus, winners will get prizes.

romantic **travel**

➤ Want to know where the best place to kiss in New York City is, or which restaurant in Los Angeles is the most romantic? Check out our Romantic Hot Spots for the scoop.

➤ Share your travel tips and stories with us on the romantic travel message boards.

romantic reading **library**

➤ Relax as you read our collection of Romantic Poetry.

➤ Take a peek at the Top 10 Most Romantic Lines!

Visit us online at

www.eHarlequin.com

on Women.com Networks